Ghosts and Bogles

Dinah Starkey

Ghosts and Bogles

pictures by
Jan Pieńkowski

HEINEMANN : LONDON

for Giles

Designed and illustrated by Jan Pieńkowski
assisted by Jane Walmsley

This edition first published 1985
First published by Good Reading Ltd 1978

SBN 434 96440 9

William Heinemann Ltd
10 Upper Grosvenor Street, London W1X 9PA

LONDON MELBOURNE TORONTO
JOHANNESBURG AUCKLAND

Printed and bound in Great Britain by
William Clowes Limited, Beccles and London

CONTENTS

All the stories in this book come from the British Isles. They are hundreds of years old and most of them have been forgotten. You can only find them in a handful of old books in a few very special libraries.

But now, by reading them, you can bring them alive again and they will live in your mind as they lived in the past.

Look carefully at the borders. Every one is different!

The Farmer and his Man

There was a farmer once who took on a new man. It was getting near harvest time and he was short-handed so he went off to the hiring fair to get some help. But he'd left it too late and the only person left to hire was little Jimmy Ridge, who was no better than a moonling and heedless with it. So he turned away, and he was walking home when a stranger came up beside him.

The farmer's dog growled and raised its hackles. And yet, there was nothing very alarming about the stranger. He was a skinny, stringy little fellow with very bright eyes. Only he had a small secret smile on his face, as if he knew something no one else did. He said to the farmer, "I hear you're looking for a new man, Benson. I'll take the job if you can meet my terms."

"Not so fast," said the farmer. "How do you know my name?"

"Never you mind. I'm a good worker, and you won't get the East Field in unless you take me on."

Like it or not, that was true, so the farmer said slowly, "What would you want?"

"Not a thing – yet. I'll work for you for a year and a day and do any mortal thing you ask of me. At the end of that time I'll tell you my terms."

"Not on your life," said the farmer. "What if you stand out for double wages?"

"I won't. It's not money I'm asking." And at that, the stranger's eyes danced wickedly, and his secret little smile widened.

"Well," said the farmer heavily. "It sounds a rum sort of arrangement to me, but beggars can't be choosers. You'd best start tomorrow."

Next morning, bright and early, the harvesters started work. They were all good men, but they soon found they couldn't match the stranger.

He scythed a swathe through the corn wide enough for a coach and horses. And the ears fell in such straight rows you'd have sworn he used a ruler. He'd got the whole field scythed by noon, and he'd done it single-handed. The others simply gaped, open-mouthed, and there wasn't one would work alongside him.

By dinner, they were mutinying. No one would sit near him.

"It's not natural," said old Tom. "No mortal man can work like that."

The farmer said nothing, but in his heart he agreed. And the animals couldn't abide the stranger either. The dogs all took to the stables and wouldn't set foot in the house when he was there.

So the farmer sent him out to sweep the byres. He got them clean as a whistle but the cows were in such a state it took all day to calm them.

Then the farmer set him on mending dry stone walls. That was a sight worth seeing. The stranger snapped his fingers and all the tumbled stones came sailing up through the air and wedged themselves in place. Solid as rock those walls were, when the stranger had finished with them.

It was all too much of a good thing. The farmer didn't like it, but he'd hired the stranger for a year and a day so he was stuck with him. He managed to find him jobs to do, but it wasn't easy because the others refused to work with him and he couldn't go near the stock without stampeding them. By haymaking time, the farmer was counting the days till the stranger was gone, but he still didn't know what pay the man would ask, and it bothered him.

"Look," said the farmer one day when it was coming up to harvest. "It's time you and me had a straight talk. You've kept your side of the bargain, and done it handsomely. I'm not denying it. But I want to know my side. What will you be asking?"

The stranger turned to him and smiled.

"Didn't I say?" he asked sweetly.

"You know full well you didn't. So let's have it out and no more games. What do you want?"

"But it must be obvious."

"Not to me it isn't," said the farmer.

"Why," said the stranger, "your soul, of course. What else? Your soul."

And then, as the farmer made some sound, he added, "And I'll have it in a week or so, too. My year's nearly up and I haven't fallen down on a job yet. You said so yourself."

"We'll see about that!" said the farmer grimly, and he strode off into the farmhouse, leaving the stranger laughing.

"Right," he said next morning, when the men gathered to learn their work. "Fred and Tom, I want the threshing floor cleared and all the root vegetables sorted. Harry, you see to the cows." He paused and turned to the stranger, who was still waiting for a job. "I want you to count the corn. Grain by grain."

"What's he got to do that for?" asked Fred, who was slow. "Seems a daft sort of job to me."

"The mice have been at it," lied the farmer stoutly. "I want to know what's missing. Now get on with it, and I'll expect the answer by sundown. A proper count, mind."

"And you shall have it," said the stranger. "Correct to the last grain."

Nobody saw anything of him for the rest of the day. He was shut up in the corn store and there were blue sparks coming out of the window. But at night he went to the farmer and said, "Ninety-four thousand, six hundred and eighty-one and a half grains. Fourteen of them are stuck down the floor boards."

"Eighty-one and a *half!*" said the farmer. "What's the half?"

"A mouse had been at one," said the stranger smoothly. "There was only half left."

"I shall check your count personally," said the farmer. "And it had better be right."

But ninety-four thousand odd grains of wheat take a bit of counting and though all the other workers lent a hand, they were up all night. When done, the tally came out exactly the same, even to the last half. When the stranger saw them next morning he laughed till he cried.

"Fred, Harry and Tom," said the farmer, rubbing his eyes, "you can take the day off. Get a bit of sleep. Lord knows, you've earned it. As for you," he added, turning to the stranger, "come outside with me. I've got another little job."

Out in the yard was a big empty water barrel. Beside it stood the farmer's wife's smallest sieve.

"I want that barrel filled," said the farmer. "Using

nothing but the sieve. Get the water from the well."

"With pleasure," said the stranger. "I'll start right away."

He put out one long bony finger, and touched the sieve. As he did so, something very funny happened to it. It quivered and then stiffened and a kind of dancing blur of light wavered around it. The farmer followed the stranger out to the well. To his disappointment, but not to his surprise, the sieve now held water. Worse than that, the water piled up in the middle like sugar on a spoon.

"Won't be long," said the stranger. "I'll have that barrel filled in two shakes. You'll see."

"It's uncanny!" said the farmer savagely. "How can I set him an impossible task when he uses magic? It's cheating!"

Old Tom said, "You could try the old iron bar trick. That's worked before against his kind."

"Good," said the farmer. "It's worth a go at least. We'll get the field ready while he's busy."

So that afternoon they collected every rusty bar they could lay their hands on and they planted them all over the East Field. It was down to hay and the grass grew up and hid the bars nicely.

Next day the farmer said, "You're to mow the East Field. Make sure your scythe's sharp."

At that, Old Tom began to cackle. But the stranger said, "Just mow the hay? Is that all?"

"That's all."

"Well, I'll do it," said the stranger, "but if you ask me, you're slipping. Surely you could have thought of something better than that."

He set off and all the farm workers trailed behind to watch. The stranger scythed smoothly through the field till he met the first iron bar. They heard the clang, and grinned, but what happened next soon wiped the smiles off their faces. There was a terrific flash, a smell of sulphur, and the bar shot up out of the ground like a rocket and sailed into the sky. As for the stranger, he winked at them, and went on.

By the time he'd dealt with four more iron bars in the same way, he was looking like the cat that got the cream. The workers trailed off to tell the farmer what had happened and he was still sitting by the kitchen fire, sunk in gloom, when there came a knock at the door. It was the old gypsy woman who sold pegs round the farms and she was bursting for a gossip.

"What's this I hear about your hired man? I thought his time was nearly up."

"Oh, Rosie, it is, and I'm at my wits' end," said the farmer. "I've got to find him something he can't do or he gets my soul. But I've tried every blessed thing I know and I can't catch him out."

"Have you tried him with a hair?" asked the gypsy. "I'll lay that beats him. Your wife's got a fine curly head of hair. Give him a strand and tell him to hammer it straight. It'd take a better man than him to do it. Now, cross my palm with silver, and I'll be on my way."

She hobbled off down the road and the farmer shouted for his wife. She had to stand still while he combed through every hair on her head until he found one at last that was curly as a pig's tail. And when he'd taken it, he called for the stranger.

"Hammer it straight," he ordered. "Not a kink in it, mind."

But the stranger was looking very black indeed. He'd quite lost his smile and his eyes were glinting.

"Who put you up to that?" he demanded. "You never thought of a trick like that on your own!"

"Maybe I did and maybe I didn't. It's none of your business. But if you can't do what I say it's no soul for you."

The stranger took a hammer and he spoke to it long and soft. The hammer glowed white hot and he raised it up and slammed it on to the hair so hard it left a hole in the table. So then he stretched it tight between two stones and hammered again, muttering strong and secret charms as he did so. But the minute he took the stones away, the hair sprang back into curl again. And then he put it on the floor, and jumped up and down on it, fists clenched, teeth grinding. But for all the effect it had, he might never have touched it.

"Impossible," he said shortly. "It can't be done."

"Then," said the farmer, "I'm afraid you'll have to go."

"I'll go!" snarled the stranger. "And may your crops rot and your cattle sicken, and may little Jimmy Ridge fire all your hayricks. And you can tell that tattle-tongued old witch that I'll be back and I'll get even with her one of these fine days."

With that he stamped his foot and was gone, leaving a drift of smoke behind him. That was the last they saw of him and none of his spiteful wishes came true. The cattle thrived, the crops flourished and little Jimmy Ridge steadied wonderfully over the next year. As for the old gypsy, she knew she was welcome to a bowl of milk and a bit of bread and cheese any time she cared to step inside the door. She lived as peacefully as you could wish and if she hasn't died she's living still.

16

The Buggane

There was once a chieftain called Broder Menine. He lived in a draughty old stronghold in Ireland and he spent money like water. He spent it on feasts and fine clothes and strings of high-bred horses and he lived like the lord he was. But the day of reckoning came and he woke up one morning without a penny to his name.

But Broder Menine wasn't the man to live on a shoe string so he decided he'd just have to get some more. He put all the family jewels in a leather sack and took ship for the Isle of Man to borrow a few thousand pounds from a man he knew there. The man was called Jarl Haco and he was so rich even his kitchen maids ate with silver spoons.

Broder Menine agreed to leave his jewels with Jarl Haco in return for a loan, but when Jarl Haco's servant brought the bags of gold aboard it struck him that there was nothing to stop him getting away with both. So he knocked Jarl Haco's servant neatly on the head, dumped him ashore, and took off back to Ireland as fast as the wind would carry him. He'd have got away with it, too, if he hadn't had a buggane on board.

Bugganes are nasty. They're not pretty beasts to start with. In fact, it's said the very sight of one will make your blood run cold. On top of that they're spiteful. A shark is a tender-hearted creature compared with a buggane in a temper. This particular buggane had only got on board by accident. It had no plans to go to sea and when it

discovered what was happening, it raised the roof. It whistled up such a storm that the fishing boats were smashed to matchsticks and the waves were the size of mountains.

The crew thought their last hour had come. When they'd taken in every rag of sail and still the ship was dashed up and down like a dead leaf, they began to pray. None prayed harder than Broder Menine. He had more reason than most.

"Oh, St Trinian," he cried, calling on the patron saint of the Isle of Man. "Only save us and I'll give all the money back."

For a moment the wind dropped and in that sudden lull the sailors could hear the cackling of the buggane. It was sitting on the mast and its little slitty eyes were screwed up with pure badness. Broder Menine took one look at it and redoubled his prayers.

"What is more," he said, "I'll give up my jewels as well. I'll use them to build a church for you if you'll just get us out of this mess."

He waited. The buggane swore long and horribly. The wind blew up again but now it had changed direction. It was driving them back into harbour. Broder Menine knew then that the saint had heard their prayers.

The buggane screeched and snapped its fingers. Instantly the ship bucked like a driven horse and every timber groaned. But still it continued to fight its way to the shore. So then the buggane drummed its heels on the mast and sent a ball of flame rocketing down from the black sky to set fire to the sails. But straight away the heavens opened and down poured a torrent which put the fire out again. The sailors let out a cheer. St Trinian was on their side.

When they got safely to land, Broder Menine hurried away to make his peace with Jarl Haco – and a hard job he had of it, too. As soon as that was done, he set out to build his church.

"Nothing but the best," he said and soon from all over England, Ireland, and even France, ships began to arrive. They carried finely seasoned timber for the beams, stained glass for the windows and velvet to make the priests' robes. Craftsmen came, too, to carve wood and stone and build the finest church in the land.

But before very long, things began to go wrong. Work finished off the night before was found undone in the morning and little fires broke out which shouldn't have started. Then some of the masons gave notice. They said there was something funny about the job and they didn't like it. One said he saw a queer looking creature lurking in the trees and it gave him the goggles.

As soon as Broder Menine heard that, he knew what was happening. The buggane was back and it was on the warpath. But he wasn't one to be beaten and so he told the workmen to wear a sprig of rowan in their caps. Rowan's good against ill-natured spirits. He hired a night watchman, too, and told him to kindle a fire of rowan wood every evening. After that the work went better and the church began to grow. But still the labourers glimpsed something queer prowling the shadows and at night the watchman heard peals of laughter outside the circle of his fire.

The church grew taller. Broder Menine brought bells in and hung them in the tower and he carved the door with flowers and fabulous beasts. When it was almost finished he gave a feast to celebrate. Ale flowed in rivers and there was an ox roasted whole. The workmen made merry till late in the evening and none feasted better than the night watchman. When he was tight as a drum with beer and roast beef, he staggered away to his little hut and fell fast asleep.

A roaring woke him. There was a brilliant light in the sky – a fitful light which danced and darted. Flames, he thought, and then he remembered he'd forgotten to light his fire of rowan wood. There was a crackling and a tremendous crash and the smell of smoke made him cough. The church was ablaze and the flames leaped high enough to touch the stars. In their light a queer slitty-eyed creature danced and capered. One of the great roof beams crashed blazing to the ground and even as he gave the alarm the watchman knew it was too late.

When they finally put the fire out, there wasn't much left of the church. It was burnt right down to the foundations, and even the stones were cracked. Broder Menine gave up the struggle right away. He'd spent all his money on that church and he simply couldn't raise enough to build a new one. He went back to Ireland and the ruins were left to crumble.

For years that church stood roofless and neglected. Nobody went near it at night. They'd all heard stories about it. Then one night Abe Hawkins got drunk.

He was a tailor, Abe Hawkins, and a boastful little man at that. So when talk came round to the ruined church, Abe was bold as a lion.

"I'd like to see the creature that'd scare *me*!" he said. "I'd give it something to remember."

Somebody laughed and Abe flushed up like a turkey cock. He was only a little fellow and touchy with it.

"Don't you believe me?"

"No," said the man who laughed. "I don't. I'll bet you

daren't stay in that church long enough to sew a pair of trousers."

"Done," said Abe, in a terrible taking. "And you'll laugh on the other side of your face by the time I'm through. Just you wait!"

He stormed off into the night to collect his needle, scissors and threads. He was in such a temper that if the buggane had turned up just then, it's doubtful who'd have come off worse. He charged up to the church, smashing through the brambles that grew all round it and, planting himself down cross-legged in the middle of the nave, began to sew.

He was still bold with drink but, as the night air cooled him, his confidence began to fade. It was dark in the church and he was working by the light of a single candle which guttered and dimmed in an unnerving fashion. Then the trees creaked more than he liked and there was a nasty scuttling noise that put him off his stroke. He began to stitch more quickly.

It was cold, too, now that he was sitting still. Cold, and quiet – except, of course, for that scuttling noise. Mice, said the tailor to himself, taking great galloping stitches. That was it. Mice.

But mice didn't pad. The tailor, who was now listening hard enough to hear a butterfly stamp, was sure there was a padding noise. It was coming nearer, too. Slap, slap, slap it went on the cold stone floor and he sewed all round the waistband in a dozen gigantic stiches. He'd come to the end of his cotton. He wrenched out the needle and rethreaded it with trembling hands and then the candle wavered as something came up behind him. It laughed.

The tailor looked out of the corner of his eye. A flat green foot stood beside his scissors. He was shivering so much he pricked himself, but he stood firm. A green hairy hand stretched out to the candle and the tailor gulped and went on sewing. But then, unable to help himself, he turned and looked full at the buggane.

"Yeeow!" he yelled and, dropping trousers, needle, thread and all, he catapulted out of that church so fast his feet scarcely touched the ground.

Back through the brambles he pelted, ripping his clothes to shreds. Behind him he heard the pound, pound, pound of the buggane's flat green feet. On to the main road he ran, puffing like a steam engine, and saw ahead of him the lights of the sea port.

Houses, he thought. People! And he put on a spurt that'd have done credit to a greyhound. But the buggane still thundered on behind, howling in a way that froze Abe's marrow.

He cast one glance back over his shoulder. The gap was widening. He was going to get away. The buggane's cries rose to a bloodcurdling pitch and it stamped its foot so hard the earth shook. Then in a frenzy of rage it plucked off its own head and hurled it full at Abe. It was as big as a coal scuttle, that head, and as hard as a coconut. It came whistling through the air and Abe skipped aside quicker than a jack rabbit. It crashed down beside him, bounced twice and lay still. And after that a wonderful stillness crept over the countryside.

And that was the end of the buggane. Abe had lost his bet and never did go back for the trousers. He left them lying in the ruined church and for all I know, you'll find them there to this day.

The London Ghost

The Reverend Dr Scott lived in a house in George Street with a marmalade cat for company. They both liked their comforts and between them they'd got the house just as they liked it with plenty of easy chairs and steak and kidney pudding every Tuesday. On a winter's evening, Dr Scott used to settle down by the fire with a glass of port and the cat on his knee as snug and cosy as a man could be. But one night, when the rain beat against the windows, a figure moved quietly across the room and sat down in a chair by the fire.

It was a man, and the sort of man who, in the normal way, would have suited Dr Scott down to the ground. He was elderly and respectable, in a black velvet gown and a long wig. His linen was spotless and his face was grave. But the clothes were fifty years out of date and he'd walked in straight through the wall.

Dr Scott sprang up and the stranger waved him back. "Please don't move," he said. "What a pleasant room.

And what a delightful cat."

He bent to stroke it but the cat, spitting green sparks, fled into the kitchen. Dr Scott took a step backwards.

"My dear sir," said the ghost, "compose yourself. There's no cause for alarm."

Dr Scott, without taking his eyes off the visitor, reached for his Bible. There were ways, he'd heard, of dealing with ghosts.

"And I don't intend to go away," it added firmly. "Not till I've said my say."

Dr Scott sank back into his chair. He swallowed hard.

"I want you to go to Wiltshire for me," said the ghost. "To take a message. Let me explain."

It settled itself more comfortably and stretched out its hand to the fire. The flames sank and then leapt up again, icy blue.

"In my life," said the ghost, "I had three sons. The eldest was as fine a boy as you could wish for, but the younger ones were wastrels and dishonest to boot. They squandered my money and broke their mother's heart so in my will I cut them both off with a shilling and left my lands to the eldest, as was right and proper."

It paused and glanced sharply at Dr Scott.

"Very well. He died and the land passed to his son – a nice enough lad who has always shown a proper respect for his grandfather. But now it has come to my notice that my younger sons, the boy's uncles, are trying to cheat him out of his rights. They have the impudence to claim that I left the land to them! And when the boy denies it, they laugh and say dead men tell no tales!"

It gave a snort of indignation and settled itself again.

"But they shall learn better before they're very much older. I have never cared for loose ends and so before I died I deeded the land to my eldest son and his children in the proper legal way."

"Well then," said Dr Scott, "there's no problem, surely? He can show them the title deeds."

"But that's the trouble. He can't. I locked them in a chest and forgot to tell him where. He will never find them unless someone helps him. And that is your task."

"Me!" cried Dr Scott. "But I don't even know him!"

"No matter. You can tell him I sent you. Now the deeds are in a chest in the lumber room under the roof and the key to the chest is on a shelf by the window. I would like you to go as soon as possible."

"I can't!" said the doctor. "And I won't. I'm not going off on a wild goose chase in the middle of winter."

"Dr Scott," said the ghost softly. "I have been very gentle with you so far. I have not appeared headless or rattling my chains. Nor have I moaned or turned the room icy cold. I have never been a man for mummery. But disagreeable though it may be, I am perfectly capable of reducing you to a gibbering imbecile and unless you agree to do as I wish immediately, I will be forced to take steps!"

A curtain billowed menacingly and an eerie whistling sounded in the chimney. The ghost advanced on Dr Scott and stretched out one cold hand.

"All right!" said Dr Scott hurriedly. "Just as you please. I'll probably catch pneumonia on the journey, but that's as fate wills. I'll take your message."

"Thank you," murmured the ghost. "And remember, the chest is in the lumber room."

Dr Scott set out the very next day, muffled against the winter air. He travelled by stage-coach and it bumped and rolled till he thought his insides would shake loose. And then, when it set him down, there was a long cold walk across frosty fields to the manor farm. Very sorry for himself he felt, as he trudged up the path, and anxious, too, because he couldn't think what he was going to say.

A young man answered the door and led him into the

kitchen, where two villainous-looking blackguards sprawled in front of the fire.

"My uncles," said the boy distantly, and they stared at Dr Scott and grunted.

He could see why the ghost thought well of its grandson. The boy took his coat to dry and gave him hot brandy and milk to drink till he was thawed right down to his toes. The lad deserved the farm, thought Dr Scott gratefully, but how he was to get the message passed was more than he could tell.

His chance came when the boy went out to the stables. Dr Scott went with him and hurriedly told him of the ghost's words. To his surprise, the boy took it very calmly.

"I dreamt about my grandfather last night," he said. "He told me someone was coming to help me. He must have meant you. We'll go up and look straight away, but we'll have to do it quietly or my uncles will hear."

They crept upstairs to the lumber room, carrying a candle to light their way. It was in chaos. There were old beds and warming pans piled up in heaps and the dust lay thick as a blanket. But in one corner, hidden behind a linen press, was a window and on the shelf beside it they found the key. And a minute or two later, the young man came on the chest, hidden by rolls of carpet.

He fitted the key with trembling fingers. It was rusty and the key was very stiff. As he raised the lid, they heard footsteps on the stair.

"Hurry!" cried Dr Scott. "They're coming."

There were piles and piles of documents, all tied together with red ribbon. They rifled through them with desperate haste and the young man gave a cry.

"This is it! Listen!"

Even as he spoke, the uncles burst into the room.

"What's going on?" cried one, but the other, quicker on the uptake, spotted the deed. He snatched it from the boy and thrust it at the candle flame. The damp paper smouldered and suddenly the room grew very cold. A faint, wispy shadow appeared in one corner. It grew thicker and began to take on a form. The uncles stood frozen as the figure of the ghost appeared.

"Enough!" it cried. "You thought you could cheat me but I swore you would fail. Now be gone before I treat you as you deserve."

It took a step forward and the uncles let out a yelp. The title deeds fluttered to the ground as they hurled themselves down the stairs and out of the house as fast as their legs could carry them. They say those villains never stopped running till they reached the sea. But as for the grandson, he took the deeds to court and no one ever doubted his claim again. And Dr Scott went back to London with such a terrible cold in the head that he allowed himself two glasses of port in front of the fire that night. Naturally, he never saw the ghost again.

The Boggart of Castle Farm

They'd always had a boggart up at Castle Farm. Lots of Yorkshire farms have them and this one had been in the family for years. The old farmer was very fond of it. It used to help him with the milking and the lambing and it did all sorts of odd jobs round the house. On winter nights it would come slipping through the kitchen door to settle on the hearth and the farmer's wife said it was better company than any dog, even if it was invisible. She gave it a big bowl of cream every night before she went to bed and in the morning she always found the bowl washed and the kitchen set to rights. It was a handy sort of boggart to have around a house.

But time passed and the old farmer and his wife died. The son, Jim, took over and married a girl from away. She hadn't much time for the farm. She didn't like the hens, and she didn't like the pigs and she most certainly didn't like the boggart.

"And you mean I'm supposed to waste good cream on

some thieving bogey man? I'll do no such thing!"

"Nay, don't take on, Flo!" said her husband. "He's come to expect it. And they're awkward creatures when they're crossed."

"I never heard such a tale!" said his wife. "Cream indeed! It'll drink skim and like it."

But as soon as the farmer came down next day he could tell that the boggart wasn't suited. It had drunk the milk all right but it hadn't done a stroke in return. The kitchen was in a pot mess and the boggart was sulking up the chimney. Not that the farmer blamed it. Skimmed milk is no treat when you're used to cream.

"You'd best give it something better tonight, love," he said. "You'll get no help if you hurt its feelings."

"Indeed I will not!" said Flo. "It's lucky to get anything."

The next night she put the bowl down once more and

the milk was so blue even the cat turned its nose up. So did the boggart. It wouldn't touch it and when they came down next day the air was thunderous.

From then on it was open war between Flo and the boggart. It pinched her and nipped her and made her jump. Every time the children settled down to their tea an invisible hand snatched the bread and butter away and spilt their milk. Every time she tidied the kitchen a whirlwind swept through, scattering flour on the floor and treacle on the door-knobs. And as if that wasn't bad enough, it used to play piggy with a shoe horn. They kept the shoe horn in a hole in the wall and the boggart would snatch it out and hurl it across the kitchen like a bullet. When it wasn't going bump in the night, that is.

Things got to such a pitch that Jim decided he'd have to get shut of it by fair means or foul. But that was easier said than done. Once you've got a boggart you're stuck with it. And this one liked Castle Farm and didn't aim to move.

First they called in the parson to cope with it, but the boggart just swung from the rafters, screeching with laughter and dropping pebbles on the Bible. Then they tried starving it out, but the boggart helped itself from the butter tubs and left smeary great footprints all over the dairy. So they tried to take no notice of it, in the hope that it'd get tired of tormenting them. But *it* didn't get tired. They did.

One night, when this had being going on for some time, the farmer called his wife and children out of the house. He put a finger to his lips and led them right down to the bottom of the garden, by the cabbage patch. He looked all round to see if anyone was near and then, leaning forward, began to speak.

"Listen," he hissed. "I'm right sick of that boggart and I'm standing it no longer. If we can't get shut of him, then we'll have to flit."

"Flit!" squealed Flo, and the farmer clapped a hand to her mouth.

"Hush!" he said. "It'll hear you. Now we'll need to do it secret like and we'd best go at night so get packed up straight away and we'll be off as soon as it's dark."

All that evening they were busy, sorting and packing. The boggart was fascinated. They could feel its scratchy fur as it leaned over their shoulders and hear the soft pad of its feet following them from room to room, while they tried to put it off the scent.

"It's a grand night for spring cleaning!" said the farmer's wife loudly. "Soon as we've got everything out of the house I'll give it a good sweep through."

She heard a disbelieving sniff from the chimney but certainly the boggart was giving no trouble and she hoped for the best. By the time they were ready to go it had made itself scarce. They loaded all their gear on to the big cart, shoved the milk churns in the back and harnessed up the horses. Just then a neighbour came along.

"Now then, Jimmy," he said. "You're never flitting?"

"I am an' all," said Jim. "That dratted boggart gives us no peace so I reckoned we'd best part company. We're going to my brother's and I'll find another farm later on."

But even as he spoke, a voice came from the milk churn. It was a raspy, boggarty sort of voice.

"That's right, Georgy," said the voice. "We're flitting." And the top of the milk churn flipped into the air, spun a full circle and clattered into place again.

The farmer froze. He clenched his fists.

"Florence!" he yelled. "Get them things back. If that boggart's come with us I'm stopping here."

And for once his wife agreed.

"It can drown in cream for all I care," she said.

So they all settled down again, the farmer, his wife, children and the boggart. And since it had got its way, peace reigned at Castle Farm ever after.

The Laying of the Pakenham Ghost

It was in the days when Parson Andrews was a young curate that the Pakenham ghost began to walk. It was a very common or garden type of ghost – so ordinary, in fact, that nobody even knew who it was. But it haunted a farmhouse near Pakenham in Suffolk, and a great nuisance it made of itself.

It was a noisy ghost. It banged and thumped and slammed doors. The farmer and his wife would hear its hollow groans overhead, always when they were getting off to sleep. When it was feeling above itself it broke china, too. It bounced it off the dresser and smashed it on the floor.

The farmer's wife, who was a good-natured woman, had a kindness for the ghost.

"Poor thing," she said. "And wouldn't you feel sorry for yourself, flapping around in a sheet with never a bite to keep out the cold?"

But the farmer, who was a harder case, said it had only

got its just deserts. "Stands to reason," he said. "It must have done something wrong during its life to get itself ghosted."

The farmer's wife ruled in that household, however, and she decided to cure the ghost by kindness.

"Make it feel at home," she explained. "Then it won't need to go racketing around waking people up."

She took to laying a knife and fork for it at every meal and chatting to it about the weather. The rest of the household didn't fancy the idea at all. The plough boy said it gave him the willies not knowing whether anything was there or not, and the farmer reckoned his pudding never lay easy. But it did seem to do the trick. For a time it looked as if the ghost was settling down.

Then the effort got too much for it. After a month or two of best behaviour it started getting up to its old tricks again. And this time the farmer put his foot down.

"I'm not having another broken night whatever you say, Mother. That ghost's got to go."

So he sent for the parson to get rid of it and the parson turned up carrying bell, book and candle and bringing with him his curate, the young Mr Andrews. He was as downy as a day-old chick, Mr Andrews, and he'd never even seen a ghost, let alone laid one.

"Now then," said old Parson Clegg, "it's all very well reading the thing down but where are you going to put it after that?"

"Put it?" said the farmer blankly.

"Of course. I can shrink it down for you but that doesn't get rid of it altogether. We need a place for it – somewhere it can't get out of . . ." He paused and, seeing the farmer still looked uncertain, added, "The usual place is a bottle."

"Ah!" said the farmer, his face clearing. "Well, I should think I could . . . "

"Oh no you don't," his wife interrupted. "I'm not having that poor thing squashed up in any old bottle. No, if you've *got* to be rid of it – and I still think it's a pity – then it can go in the spare room wardrobe, which is nice and roomy."

"But I keep my Sunday best in there!" protested the farmer.

"For shame!" said his wife. "Grudging the poor creature a decent home. The cupboard it shall be."

With that settled, the laying began. They had a hard time with that ghost. It liked the farmhouse and having its own knife and fork and it didn't want to go. Parson Clegg read till his voice was hoarse and had the young curate spinning round like a teetotum, lighting candles and putting them out, ringing bells and swinging dishes of sweet-smelling herbs. But the old parson had read down a lot of ghosts in his time and before the day was out he'd got it shrunk to the size of a field mouse and laid it in the cupboard with the key on the outside. The farmer papered the door over so neatly you'd scarcely know it was there, and nothing was heard of the ghost for a long time.

Years went by and the house changed hands. A new couple took it over, who came from Norfolk. Nobody told them about the ghost because they were a nice young couple and nobody wanted to bother them. But one day as the wife – Alice Willcox, her name was – dusted out the bedroom, she happened to notice a bump in the wallpaper. It was where the key stuck out, in fact, but she didn't know that. She called one of the maids, who'd been there in the old farmer's time, and asked what it was.

"A cupboard, ma'am," said the maid unwillingly.

"Well I never!" said Alice. "Help me to pull off the wallpaper then."

"No!" said the maid. "I wouldn't do that!"

"Why ever not?" Alice was stripping off the paper as

she spoke, and she'd found the lock.

"Don't! Leave it alone!"

But Alice had got the key free and she was turning it.

"There's a ghost, ma'am!"

"A ghost? What nonsen. . . "

But as she spoke she opened the door and with a whoosh and a blast of freezing air, the ghost got out. A cloud of mist formed in the air, whirled and went streaking upstairs. There was a furious banging and a crash. It was back in business.

Down flew the plough man to the vicarage to root out the parson.

"Come quick!" he panted. "The ghost's got out and it's breaking up the house!"

Young curate Andrews, who was now Parson Andrews, and quite a few years older, sighed. He remembered that long hard day with the bell and the candles. But he got his things together and ran.

The ghost was bashing about in the attic and the dairy maid was having hysterics. There wasn't a whole piece of china in the house.

"Put it back at once!" cried Alice Willcox. "It's gone mad!"

The ghost let out a howl like a banshee and Parson Andrews gritted his teeth.

"Back in the cupboard?" he asked wearily.

"No," she said. "Not there. It'll only get out again. And I must say," she added, "it was a pretty silly place to put a ghost in the first place. Asking for trouble."

"I did hear tell," put in the maid, "of a ghost being locked up in a clock once. Now we've got that old grandfather clock down in the hall and it's never gone right since the old farmer knocked it over."

"The very thing," said Parson Andrews. "I'll put it in the pendulum."

"Yes," said Alice Willcox, "and before you know it, someone'll come along and open it up again. No. You take the pendulum and put it somewhere safe."

"Down the well," said Parson Andrews. "Now, may I begin?"

And so the ghost was laid. Parson Andrews wrestled with it all afternoon but, as night was falling, the ghost gave a final howl and squeezed into the pendulum slick as butter. And they took it and dropped it right to the bottom of the well and put the cover on the well and a stone on top of *that*.

"And if it gets out now," said Parson Andrews, "I'll eat my hat."

Time passed and Alice Willcox grew tired of farming, with the mud and the pigs and a ghost down the well. So she and her husband went back to Norfolk and they sold the farm to old Mr Greenman, who'd had his eye on it for years. He knew all about the ghost, of course, but he rented it to a man called Bateson and he didn't let on.

Before Bateson had been in a month, he decided to drag the well. You'd be surprised at the things that were down there. Bateson found a rusty tea kettle, two buckets, half a dozen bed-springs and, last of all, a dull metal object that looked like a pendulum. And that pleased him very much because he'd noticed the clock in the hall didn't work and this had annoyed him. He took it back to the house, cleaned it up and hung it inside the clock again. Then he gave the screw a couple of turns and set it going.

There was a groan of rusty cogs creaking into action. The clock gave one slow, heavy tick and then, with a swoop and a cloud of smoke, the ghost was out of the clock and racing through the kitchen. There was a rattle and a violent cry and before Bateson knew what had hit him, the ghost was back.

He couldn't make head nor tail of it. Nobody told *him* the house was haunted. But he was no man's fool and he had the stable lad out and down to the vicarage before you could say Jack Robinson.

Old Parson Andrews was shaky now, and rather deaf, but he didn't need telling twice. Not where the ghost was concerned.

"This is too much!" he said. "Sheer carelessness! Am I to spend the rest of my days bundling that ghost back into captivity? And where am I to put it this time? In a cheese cloth, I suppose. Or perhaps your master would prefer the four poster?"

"Dunno, sir," said the stable lad woodenly.

"Very well. But I warn you, boy, this is the last time!"

He hobbled down to the farm, clutching his bell, book and candle. The ghost was racketing about in the kitchen and old Parson Andrews fairly let fly at it.

"Hold your peace, sir!" he stormed. "As if you haven't caused enough trouble already. And as for you, farmer," he turned on Bateson, "I must say you'd have done better to leave things alone. Still, it's no good crying over spilt milk. I can put it down the well again, but if I do, I want it sealed up properly. I really cannot go through this performance again."

"Oh, I'll seal it up, sir," said Bateson grimly. "I'll block the well with good solid stone, and that's a promise."

"Good!" said Parson Andrews and he rounded on the ghost. He hunted it through the house, trapped it in a corner, and then drove it backwards, step by step, till it was hard up against the well. It didn't stand a chance. The parson was in such a fury he could have tackled the Wild Hunt single-handed. He got it into the well in ten minutes flat. There was a bad-tempered yelp and the ghost was gone.

"I leave it in your hands," he told Bateson. "But if you

take my advice you'll use mortar, good and thick."

But in the end, Bateson did better. He filled in the well as he had promised and he built a summer-house on top. It was a funny looking summer-house because the walls were six foot thick and the door was triple bolted.

"But it'll stand till Judgement Day," he said. "And as for getting out, I'd just like to see the varmint try!"

And it never did. Not so far, anyway. But if you happen to be round Pakenham way and you come across a very solid looking summer-house . . . watch your step.

Whuppity Stoorie

There was once a goodwife who lived with her man on a croft called Kittlerumpit. It was only a small holding but they had a fine vegetable patch and a pig and they got by well enough. But one sad day came when the man upped and disappeared. He vanished into thin air and whether he went to seek his fortune, or got taken by the press gang, nobody could say. The fact of the matter was, he'd gone for good and his wife was left to fend for herself and for her little son, too.

She had a hard time of it, poor woman. There were plenty of people to sigh and say it was a shame, but few enough who'd lift a hand to help her. She was left to tend the garden and the pig and work the land as best she could and there was no money coming it. She lived on porridge and well water, and there were times when there was little enough of them.

But the woman had one great hope. The pig was breeding and she looked forward to the day when she'd have lots of little piglets to sell at market. When that time came she'd have money in her pocket again and all would be well. At night, when she was very tired, she'd lie in bed and plan all the things she'd buy – a bonnet for the baby and a big sack of flour and a bag of sugar for high days and holidays.

But it's a mistake to count your piglets before they're born, as she very soon found out. She went down to the pigsty one morning with a bucket of scraps and there was the sow, flat on its back, with its four trotters sticking up to the sky. It was grunting and groaning as if its last day had come and it didn't take a vet to tell her it was as near dead as made no odds.

She ran into the house to fetch warm water and milk and anything else she thought might help. She tried every trick she knew to get the pig back on its feet again but it wasn't a bit of good. It grew steadily weaker and by midday she knew it was going to die, piglets and all. And if the pig died, what in the world would become of her and her baby?

It was the last straw. She sat on the wall of the sty, flung her apron over her head, and cried as if her heart would break. She cried till her throat ached and she was just beginning to think that pig or no pig, she'd have to get on with her work when she heard footsteps tapping across the yard. Quick, determined footsteps they were, and they came trick-track, trick-track over the cobbles neat as a dancer. Well, her's was a lonely croft and nobody ever came near, so she wiped her eyes and looked up to see who had come visiting.

It was a lady. She was an old lady but she held herself stiff as a poker and she didn't look the kind who stood any nonsense from anybody. She wore a green gown with a white apron, snowy clean and edged with lace. On her head was a tall beaver hat and in her hand a shiny cane.

Altogether, she looked as neat and proper a body as the goodwife had ever seen and she found herself smoothing her hair and settling her collar to make herself fit to receive her.

"Woman," said the old lady briskly, "why are you crying? I could hear you half way down the lane."

The woman rose and dropped a little curtsey. The visitor was the kind who made you mind your manners.

She said, "I'm the unluckiest soul alive."

"Fiddle!" snapped the visitor. "Give me no fairy tales for I've no patience with them. Tell me your troubles and no more flim-flam."

"It's the honest truth!" said the goodwife, rather nettled. "Look at my sow. She's dying and if she goes it's all up with me and my little one too."

"Poppycock!" said the old lady. "I know fine she's sick *and* I know your goodman's left you too, but there's no call for that hullaballoo. Where there's a will there's a way. Now what'll you give me if I cure your sow?"

"Anything!" said the woman. "Anything in the world."

"Very well. Now get away from that sty and let me through. And put your apron straight while you're about it. You've been letting yourself go, my girl. You look like a scarecrow."

So the woman made way and her visitor marched into the sty. She looked sternly at the pig and felt it all over. Then she began to mutter under her breath. The goodwife couldn't catch most of it but she heard the old lady say "Pitter patter, holy water," and then a great long rigmarole that made no sense at all.

"You're in my light," said the old lady sharply. "Move over. And you can get those straws out of your hair while you're about it."

She took out a stout black bag, very clean and well polished. From it she drew a bottle of oil and she rubbed it into the pig's ears, its tail and its hooves. A strong, spicy smell filled the air and the pig sneezed.

"Get up," said the old lady.

The goodwife wasn't in the least surprised when the pig heaved itself to its feet. The old lady had that kind of voice. But she was very pleased and greatly relieved, especially as the pig waddled over to the trough and began eating as if it had been starved for a week.

"And now," said the old lady, "I'll not say no to a dish of tea. Strong, mind, and see you warm the teapot. And I'll need a towel to wash my hands – a soft one."

Well, the goodwife would have given her the moon and stars she was so grateful. She served the tea on the best lace tablecloth which only came out at Hogmanay and she snatched a minute to comb her hair, too, and put on a fresh apron.

They drank their tea like gentlefolk and neither of them was rude enough to mention payment straight off, but when the lady had finished and wiped her fingers daintily, she said, "Now then, my fee."

"Oh yes," said the goodwife. "Of course. Not that anything could repay you. Would you like one of the piglets? You can have the pick of the litter."

"I would not," said the lady. "No, I'm not greedy. I like to spread a little happiness when I pass and I ask small enough reward. You'll not find me unreasonable. All I'll want is your little son."

"*What?*" cried the goodwife.

"Well, it's not much to ask. He's no bigger than a minnow and he's not a bit of use to you. More of a burden. No, that's my bargain and I'll thank you to hand over."

But the goodwife wasn't listening. She'd set up such a wail you could hear her half way to England and she was rocking back and forth with the tears streaming down in rivers.

"Stop that din!" said the lady sharply. "I'm not deaf. A bargain's a bargain and you agreed to it of your own free will. I kept my word. Now you keep yours."

"Never!" said the goodwife. "You tricked me."

"I did not. Now I'm not able to take the child straight off. But I'll be back three days from now and I'll want him ready by then – and clean."

"Is there no other way?"

"None," said the old lady smugly. "Unless you guess my name. If you do that, you can keep him. But you won't, so have him waiting. And now I'll bid you good day."

With that she tripped off across the cobbles with her heels clack, clack, clacking at every step. But as for the goodwife, she cried herself to sleep and nothing would comfort her. Even the sight of the pig, pink and rosy in its sty, only set her crying louder.

She spent the whole of the next day sobbing and hugging her child till she nearly squeezed the breath out of him. But by the second day she grew so weary of her misery she decided to go out. There were a hundred jobs to do and she couldn't spare the time, but what did the chores matter if she was going to lose her baby? So she put on her shawl and went.

There was a wood close by the croft and she picked her way along the track, carrying the baby, until she came to an old quarry, covered with gorse. A spring bubbled up beside it and close by was a little clearing. There she heard the sound of a spinning wheel and somebody singing.

The goodwife was curious. To her knowledge, nobody lived in the wood, and anyway, who'd hump a spinning wheel all the way through the gorse when they could sit at home and spin? So she crept closer and looked through the branches, hushing her baby in case he made a sound. And there was the lady, sitting very straight, and spinning the finest, softest thread the goodwife had ever seen. She wore a crisp white cap now, and her boots were polished like glass. She worked the wheel at a tremendous rate and as she worked, she sang in a small sharp voice,

"Whuppity Stoorie is my name,
She never knew it when I came."

And then she fell to laughing so hard she could scarcely spin and it wasn't the kind of laughter that's good to hear, either.

"So!" thought the goodwife. "That's it, is it? I'll see her laugh on the other side of her face before I'm done!" And she stole back through the wood, soft as a cat, and set about her work with a light heart because now all would be well.

Now the goodwife was a cheerful woman when she wasn't burdened with troubles, and fond of a joke, so she decided to play a trick on the lady. When the time came, she hid the baby behind the door, pulled her cap askew, and twisted her face up as if she was on the edge of tears. Then she waited.

Sure enough, on the dot of the appointed time, there came a knock at the door. In marched the lady, very neat and brisk, and with a nasty glint in her eye.

"Well?" she said. "Where's the boy?"

The goodwife wrung her hands and, falling on her knees cried, "Oh spare him! Take the sow instead."

"Sow indeed!" said the lady. "I didn't go to all that trouble for a pig. I want your boy and I've no time to waste. Get him quickly and I'll be on my way."

"Oh, not the boy!" cried the goodwife, howling worse than ever. "Let him be and take me instead!"

"The woman's mad!" said the lady. "What would I want with you, for heaven's sake? It's your child I'm after and I'll have him, if you please."

Well, the goodwife was ruffled by that because she

thought she was worth something at least, and more use than a baby by any reckoning. So she bounced up off the ground, made a curtsey, and said crossly, "I'm sure I'm worth little enough to the likes of you but I'm not such a good-for-nothing as all that, for I know your name, Mistress Whuppity Stoorie!"

At that name, the lady almost jumped out of her skin. Her face pinched up and two little wisps of smoke came out of her nostrils.

"So!" she said, and stamped her foot hard enough to shake the house.

"So!" said the goodwife, snatching up her child. "And now be off with you, for I've kept my side of the bargain."

Then Whuppity Stoorie let out a screech like a barn owl and swept off down the path as if the devil himself was after her. There were scorch marks on the floor where her foot touched it and the goodwife never did get them off, though she scrubbed till her hands were sore. But she didn't care because the baby was safe, and so was she. And the pig farrowed next week and had ten splendid piglets. She made a pretty penny at market and ended up with a nice little nest egg. So she went singing about her work and she was never troubled by Whuppity Stoorie again.

Black Annis

Black Annis lived in the Danehills. Her face was blue and her teeth were sharp and she ate people. She only came out at night and then you could hear her grinding her teeth when she was miles away. It gave people a chance to lock their doors. They didn't have too many windows in those parts because she used to stretch her skinny arms through and help herself to babies. They didn't have their fires in the middle of the room either. They put them in a corner, as far from the outside as they could get, to make it harder for her to reach.

In one cottage in the Danehills there lived three young brothers – Jim, Jem and Jonathan, and a sad little family they were. Their own mother had died and their father married again, hoping to have someone to look after them. But that was a mistake. Their new stepmother didn't care tuppence for the children. She was cruel and idle and spent most of the day in bed. When she *was* up and about she shouted at them all the time. They were made to do all the washing and the cleaning and the scrubbing, and she grudged every penny their father spent on them. The neighbours said it was a crying shame but that didn't help the boys.

Well, the year went by and Christmas time came. There wasn't any Christmas tree in that house, nor presents either. It was bitter cold and the children couldn't seem to get warm whatever they did. So they sat in the kitchen, huddled together, while Jim, the eldest, told them a story to cheer them up.

All of a sudden, the stepmother heaved herself out of her warm bed.

"Out!" she said. "I'm getting up. Stir your lazy stumps and get some wood in."

Jim got up without a word and went to the woodshed. But their father had been busy the day before and he'd forgotten to chop any.

"There's none left," he said. "It's all used up."

"Then go and find some!" yelled the stepmother. "And fast!"

The brothers looked out of the door. It wasn't late, but the light was beginning to fail and the cold grey winter dusk was closing in around the house.

"But it'll be dark in a minute!" said Jem.

"Well?" cried the stepmother harshly. "What of it?"

"Black Annis comes out at night. She might get us."

"She's welcome. And good riddance I say. Now be off with you and look sharp about it."

There was no help for it. The boys bundled themselves into their coats and dragged out into the cold. It was a dark, cheerless sort of afternoon. Yellow lights shone warmly in every cottage window but there wasn't a soul to be seen out of doors. Jonathan, the little one, began to cry.

"Don't take on, Jonty. We'll take care of you," said Jem.

"She'll get us," he sniffed. "You see!"

"Not she," said Jim bravely. "Not if we're quick."

So they set to and started gathering firewood as fast as they could go. But there wasn't much about and somehow they found themselves going further and further away from the houses. It wasn't quite dark yet, but the light was going fast.

"Hurry!" said Jim to Jem.

"Can't!" he gasped. "My fingers are frozen."

They'd got right up to the little wood on top of the hill by now, and they were working slower and slower because of the dark and the cold. Their bundles kept slipping and they had to stop to put them straight.

"Oh, come on!" said Jem at last. "That'll do. Let's be off before something happens."

"It's all right," said Jim. "It's Christmas Eve, don't forget. She'll not be out tonight. If she hears the church bells, she's dead. No, she'll be holed up safe underground."

"Maybe," said Jem. "But the sooner we're home, the better I'll like it. Let's run."

But they couldn't because of the firewood. So they just hoisted it on their backs and plodded off home as fast as they could. A long way it was, too, and the sun was all but gone. Just a bright rim showed above the fields. And then, in the stillness, they heard the gnashing of teeth.

"It's her!" cried Jonty. "She's coming."

"But she's supposed to be safe underground, away from the bells!"

"Well, she must have forgotten," said Jim.

He'd got his hand in his pocket and he was burrowing about among the bits of string and old nails.

"I've got a holed stone here," he said. "And if I look through that, I can see what she's up to."

It was a flint, worn with water. He held it up to his eye.

The others couldn't see a thing but dark and trees, but as soon as he looked through it, he saw her coming. She was very small and far off yet, but her long sharp nose was twitching and she sniffed her way along like a hound on the scent. And Jim knew what scent she followed. She was after them.

"Run!" he shouted. "Run for your lives! Never mind the firewood!"

He snatched up one of Jonty's hands and Jem took the other and they raced him off down the hill so fast his feet scarcely touched the ground. But it was full dark now, and the ground was glassy with frost. They couldn't keep up that breakneck pace. Like it or not, they had to slow down. Behind them they heard the grinding teeth again.

"Look through the stone, Jim," gasped Jem.

So he looked and there she was, much nearer this time. Her great flat feet pounded over the ploughed fields and her hair was flying wild. She was only a mile away.

"Come on!" said Jim and seized Jonathan's hand again. They ran like rabbits, but she was still gaining. Then they heard a yell.

"Who was that?" said Jonty.

"It's Stepmother!" said Jim. "She must have come out to look for us and Black Annis got her."

"Good," said Jim. "That'll keep her busy."

But they went on running for all that because they knew she wouldn't stop for long.

Sure enough, a few minutes later they heard the slap, slap, slap of her feet. The stepmother was too bitter for her taste so she hadn't stopped to make a meal of her. She wasn't more than half a mile off, and she was coming quickly.

"Drop your coat, Jonty," called Jim, "and run for home."

Jonty bolted and when Black Annis reached the coat

she fell flat on her face and grazed her shins. She screeched and ran back to her cave to get a hank of cobweb to stop the bleeding, because if a witch bleeds, she dies.

Jim and Jem went like the wind but she was back again and after them in no time at all. And they were tired out. When she was only a quarter of a mile off they both dropped their coats.

"And if that doesn't hold her," gasped Jim, "we're done for."

Jem nodded, too spent to speak. Behind them they heard a scream of rage as she went sprawling. But now they put on a fresh spurt because ahead of them they saw the cottage. And their father stood at the door, holding his big axe.

Black Annis was up and after them again. She was close at their heels. Jem felt her bony fingers clawing at his shoulder and then his father hurled the axe full in the witch's face. She screeched and at that very moment, the church bells rang out and she fell down dead.

But as for the children, they went inside. Their father had built up the fire and they drew the curtains and made toast for tea. And the church bells pealed all night because the witch was dead.

Tregeagle's Ghost

Down in Cornwall, where the sea runs fierce and fast, there lived a wicked squire called Tregeagle. He was a rogue and a liar and a murderer, too, if you could believe the stories. He beat his servants and terrified his tenants and he went rampaging round the countryside looking for chances for fresh wickedness. So when his people learnt that he was on his deathbed, there wasn't a soul to weep for him. They thought it served him right.

But Tregeagle was no fool and he knew that if he died with all his sins on him, he'd go straight to hell. So he called in the church and offered gold in rivers to anyone who'd save his soul. There were thirty monks from St Albans priory gathered round his bed, chanting their heads off, and candles burning like all the stars in heaven. And indeed, when the demons came to snatch his soul, the chanting and the candles held them back and they retired baffled. But it was a close run thing and many of the monks were seen tottering away, wiping their brows and calling for brandy to revive them.

Well, Tregeagle was buried very decently with coal-black horses, and a slap-up ham tea. All the servants were put in mourning and everyone heaved a sigh of relief. But his wickedness outlived him. When the lawyers came to go through his papers they found he'd been mixed up in the affairs of a young man from Bodmin and there'd been skulduggery in it somewhere.

No one could exactly make it out. It seemed he'd taken the young man's lands, sold them to someone else and gone off with the profits. But he'd covered his tracks so cleverly there wasn't a shred of proof. Except that the young man had lost his estate and the new owner, who'd paid good money for it, wasn't going to hand it back without a struggle.

So there was a court case. The young man stood up and swore on his honour that the land was his, and the new owner insisted it was his, bought and paid for. As for the judge, he couldn't make head nor tail of the case, because wicked old Tregeagle had cooked the books so thoroughly.

The last witness had been heard and the judgement was near at hand. Everyone could see it would go badly with the young man, and he knew it too. He was desperate to prove his case and, just as the judge prepared to sum up, he said, "My Lord, I would like to call an extra witness. His name is Jan Tregeagle."

There was a murmur of astonishment and then a hush. The courtroom grew cold. Darkness filled the air. When it cleared, Tregeagle stood before them. He was dressed in black and a cloud of demons hovered around him like horseflies. He looked as insolent as ever but, in a loud, clear voice, he gave his evidence. And with nothing to lose, he admitted every last thing. The young man's case was proved completely.

But it was one thing to call Tregeagle up, and quite another to get rid of him. When he'd finished, the judge thanked him courteously and invited him to step down. But he stayed where he was. The judge wound up the case and awarded the land to the young man, but Tregeagle didn't budge. The young man went rejoicing home and the judge turned to a case of cattle stealing, but Tregeagle stood there still, solid as a rock. What's more, it looked as if he'd stop there for good.

The judge called in the prior and they put their heads together.

"It's clear enough what's happened," said the prior. "Our prayers saved him from hell, but he's far too wicked to go to heaven. And the demons are just waiting for a chance to get him. To put it bluntly, we're stuck with him."

"Not me!" said the judge. "Not in my courtroom. I want rid of him and I want it fast."

The prior shrugged unhappily. "We could try setting him a task, I suppose. Put him to work doing something impossible to purge his soul."

So they went back into court. Everyone had gone home now and the place was deserted, except for Tregeagle. He glared at them from the witness box with such fury that the prior reached for his cross. But the judge was made of sterner stuff.

"Now then, my man," he said. "I can't have you cluttering up my courtroom any longer, so I'll thank you to be off."

Tregeagle sneered and snapped his fingers rudely. "*That* to your court!" he said. "I'd like to see you shift me."

"That won't be necessary," said the prior. "You're to take yourself off to Dozmary Pool as a penance and you will stay there till you've baled it dry."

Tregeagle burst into loud coarse laughter. "That pool's the size of a lake!" he said. "And what am I supposed to bale it with – a horse trough?"

"No," said the prior. "I'll give you a limpet shell with a hole in it. If you agree, you will purge your sins. And if you don't . . . " he continued, raising his voice slightly, "I'll let all the devils of hell in here and I won't raise a finger to help you."

There was a thunderous silence. Tregeagle fumed and swelled till he almost filled the courtroom. Then, with a bellow of rage, he vanished. The first of his labours was begun.

But he made very heavy weather of it. As fast as he baled out the water with his limpet shell, down came the rain and filled the pool again. And to make matters worse, the demons got to hear about the bargain and determined to stop him by fair means or foul. They raised the most almighty storms to drive him from his task. Winds howled round him, rain lashed him, and hailstones the size of duck eggs pelted his head, but he stuck it out, cursing furiously.

And then one night they sent such a storm that the murky water rose up against him. The wind snatched his hat away and carried it to the edge of the moor and, to cap it all, it began to sleet. Tregeagle could stand no more and, with a blinding oath, he slammed down his shell and ran.

Now came the demons' chance. They closed on him in a pack and chased him three times round the pool. But he broke free and raced across the dark countryside till he came to a lonely chapel. Just as the demons were about to pounce, he jammed his head through the east window and bawled, "Now try and get me, you miserable scum! Take one step into this holy place and you'll be scorched to cinders! Be off and find someone else to torment."

It was true what he said. The demons retreated to a safe distance and a hermit, disturbed by all the hullaballo, came out to see what had happened. It was a dreadful how d'you do. The ghostly bottom half of Tregeagle stuck out of the east window while from the inside, his enormous grinning face appeared, wedged tightly in the window frame. And his yells of triumph were fit to cave the roof in.

But it was out of the frying pan, into the fire for him, as he very soon found out. The hermit was forever praying in the chapel and the sound of those prayers was anguish to his graceless soul. And when Sunday came, and the faithful gathered for service, he screamed and bawled so horribly they had to give it up as a bad job. It was hard on the hermit too, because he couldn't keep his mind on higher things, with a great ugly phantom head glowering at him through the window. So after a bit, he went to St Petroc.

"It's getting me down," he said. "You'll have to get rid of that hooligan somehow. I can't cope any longer."

"Fair enough," said St Petroc. "We'll find him other work to do."

He called at the chapel next day to set the new task, and it was even worse than the old one. "You're to go to Padstow," he said, "and twist the sand there into rope. And not one second's rest can you take till you've succeeded."

"Sand into rope!" grumbled Tregeagle. "It can't be done."

"Exactly," said the saint. "Now off you go."

There was a rushing wind and a pop like a cork coming out of a bottle as Tregeagle's head shot out of the window. Next minute he was on Padstow sands, starting his new task. But you can imagine what it was like. Every time he got a handful of sand together, the wind blew it away. When, after great effort, he did manage to get a grain or two to stick together, the sun dried them and they'd fall apart again. And being an impatient sort of soul, he didn't take it kindly. He bellowed and bawled and roared with temper until it drove the people of Padstow up the wall. The noise continued night and day and none of them got a wink of sleep. At last they went to St Petroc and complained.

"Why us?" they demanded. "What have we ever done to deserve him? Send him to Penzance. They're an evil living lot there by all accounts."

Well, the saint listened to everything they said and he agreed they'd cause for complaint. He didn't send Tregeagle to Penzance, but he packed him off to Barippa to sweep the beach clear of sand. He was to keep on till he'd got down to solid rock. But the sand at Barippa is fathoms deep and the sea washes fresh drifts on to the beach with every tide. So though Tregeagle worked like a hero and shifted sand by the ton, the beach never grew less. And the demons were at him morning, noon and night, teasing and tormenting him to make him stop. He paid no heed until one day, as he was carrying a great load of sand away, one of the braver sort stuck out a foot and tripped him up.

Down he went, flat on his face, and the mountain of sand he bore crashed back into the sea. It spread into a vast sandbar, right across Helston creek, and blocked the harbour mouth completely. Helston had been a thriving little port before, but that was the end of their seafaring days. Not surprisingly, the townspeople were furious.

"We're not standing for it any more!" they said. "It's not very nice having a ghost stalking about at the end of the creek, but we put up with it and never a word of complaint. *And* we put up with the noise and never knowing where he'd tip his loads. But this is too much and we want him out."

So out he went. St Petroc sent him to Land's End to heap boulders.

"And surely to goodness," he thought to himself, "Tregeagle can't do any harm there."

And perhaps he was right because Tregeagle hasn't budged since. He still makes a terrible commotion and you can hear him crashing around to this very day, when the wind's in the right direction. If the demons don't get him first, he'll be there till Doomsday. But he'd never give in. And good luck to him is what I say.

McGregor and the Kelpy

There was a kelpy that haunted the shores of Loch Ness. It took the form of a black horse, but its coat had a greenish shine to it, like that dark seaweed you find on rocks. And it was wicked. It waited by the water's edge for passing travellers and drowned them deep in the loch.

Now the beast had the patience of Job, but strangers were few and far between and it must have grown tired of waiting about because one night Ian McGregor's daughter came running into their cottage with a face as white as cheese.

"Bolt the door!" she gasped. "It's after me!"

McGregor was a slow-moving sort of man, who didn't panic easily, but he got the bolt up like greased lightning because he could see the state she was in.

"Who?" he said. "What's the matter, lass?"

But the girl was sobbing so much she could hardly speak, and it was a long time before they could get the story out of her.

It seemed she'd been walking by the edge of the loch, looking for driftwood, when she saw a young man coming towards her.

"Oh, and he was handsome!" she said. "The bonniest man I ever saw. But strange looking, mind. And he knew my name. I thought that was funny because I knew fine I'd never seen him before. Well, we got talking and he was telling me all kinds of queer things about the loch – things I'd never dreamt of, though I've lived here all my life. And it was all so interesting that it was dinner time before we knew it, and he shared my bannock and cheese. Then he put his head in my lap and I began to comb his hair."

She gave a little gasp and then continued.

"But his hair was wet," she said. "Dripping wet, though I knew for a fact he hadn't been near the water since morning. He couldn't have been, you see, because he'd been talking to me. And the comb was full of sand and tiny pebbles. Then I saw he was watching me. He was laughing. Of course I knew fine what he was then, and why I'd never had a sight of him before. But I said 'You're all in a tangle, aren't you?' and carried on as if I hadn't noticed. I didn't dare let him know I'd guessed for fear of what he'd do. I combed as softly and slowly as I could and bit by bit, his head felt heavier. His eyes were closing. But still I didn't stop. I went on till I was sure he was fast asleep and then I put his head down and I slipped away as quietly as ever I could. He didn't stir and for all I know he's asleep there still, but he knows my name and he knows where I live and he'll be after me, I know he will. Whatever am I going to do?"

At that she fell to crying again and McGregor stared into the fire.

"Whisht, lassie, it'll be all right," said her mother. "He can't get in here. You're safe now."

But Mairi wept on and would not be comforted while

her father glared into the fire. At last he said, "I'll see you safe, Mairi, and that's a promise. Elspeth, fetch my dirk. I'm off out and I'll not be back till late. You're to put rowan round the doors and windows so the beast can't get in. I'll teach it to play tricks with my daughter or my name's not Ian McGregor."

With that, he strode out into the twilight, dirk in hand. He went off down to the lake to search for the kelpy, but the dark was gathering and before long he began to doubt if he'd find it. He was just wondering whether to go home and try again next morning when before him, standing by the water, he saw a tall black horse. There was no one to be seen for miles around but the horse was saddled and bridled as if for riding and it watched him from the corner of its eye.

McGregor stood still and waited. The horse snorted and its bridle jingled in the still air. It looked ordinary enough and yet there was something not quite right about it. Its coat shone like seaweed and the set of its head was knowing.

It sidled closer, while McGregor eased his dirk from the sheath. It drew nearer and with it came the smell of lake water and a coldness. Then it was upon him, jostling him, forcing him back towards the loch. But it made no sound.

McGregor stumbled and almost lost his footing. The animal reared up, seizing its chance, and lashed at him with hooves as sharp as knives. Its ears were flat again its head and its eyes were wicked. He ducked, shielding himself as best he could and reached up to snatch at its bridle. As everyone knew, the power of a water horse lay in its bit. Without it, it was helpless.

But it was no easy task to grasp the bit, let alone cut it free. The kelpy forced him back and back, to the very edge of the loch, while McGregor hung on like grim death. He'd managed to slash through the leather on one side when it reared up over him, baring its teeth. The black water lay below him, deep and still and cold as death. He teetered, flung out a hand to save himself, and with the sudden strain the bit broke free. The horse screamed and flung itself into the loch.

McGregor sat down on a stone to get his breath back. He knew this wasn't the end by a long chalk. He thrust the bit deep in his pocket and waited for the next move. It was almost dark. He could just see the gleaming ripples on the water and presently, in the distance, a dark head broke the surface and came arrowing towards him. A young man pulled himself out of the water and came striding across the shore.

"Give it back," he said curtly.

McGregor shook his head.

"It's mine," said the young man. "You stole it."

Still McGregor made no reply and the young man took a step forward. His hair gleamed in the darkness.

"I'll give you gold," he said coaxingly. "I'll give you your heart's desire if you'll only let me have it."

"I don't want gold," said McGregor. "I want to see my family at peace and that they never will be while you have your bit."

"What will you do with it?"

"I'll keep it safe where you can never reach it."

The young man's fists clenched.

"Just you try!" he shouted. "Just try and get it home even. You'll never get it across the threshold for I'll be there, barring the way. And I'll have it back if it's the last thing I do!"

He wheeled, and was gone, running like a deer across the heather. A patch of cloud covered the moon and when it cleared there was no sign of him. But a black horse thundered across the glen, heading for McGregor's croft.

It was some time later when McGregor reached home.

Sure enough, he found the water horse waiting on the threshold, and he knew he hadn't a chance of getting past. Every window in the house was candlelit and the doors were decked with rowan. He could see his wife and daughter peering anxiously through the glass but the water horse pawed the ground and he was on the outside, in the dark.

Mairi cried, "Give him the bit, Father. He says he won't move until you do."

But McGregor gripped it all the tighter and began inching round to slip in behind the water horse. He had his hand on the door-knob when it struck at him so sharply that he gasped. Its ears flattened and it drove him backwards. His wife had got the big iron cooking pot and she hurled it at the kelpy to try and drive it away. But though the blow fell square and the beast squealed with pain and fury it would not give way. It stood four square in front of the door and McGregor could see no way of getting by.

He looked at the house, protected by rowan, and he knew that if he could only get the bit inside he'd be safe. And suddenly he knew how to do it.

"Elspeth!" he cried. "Catch hold!"

The bit flew up to her window, glittering in its flight. The horse reared in a vain attempt to seize it and Elspeth's hands stretched out, fumbled for a second, and then had it safe.

"Be off!" she shouted. "The bit's out of your reach now and you must do as I say."

She waved it in triumph and the water horse was still, watching. Suddenly it tossed its mane and galloped away, running like the wind. It never stopped till it reached the loch and that was the last the McGregors saw of it. There was no more trouble for them after that, nor for anyone else. And there never has been, to this very day.

The Dauntless Girl

Nothing frightened the dauntless girl. She was only a little snip of a thing, no bigger than a sparrow, but she was bold as a lion. She was a very busy, brisk sort of girl with no time for nerves or fancies. She had a job with a farmer near her home and she was worth her weight in gold. She was so quick and handy she did the work of three girls and made a right good job of it.

The farmer was a friendly fellow and he liked to have his cronies in from time to time. The beer would go round and the stories would get taller, and the dauntless girl sat in the kitchen mending socks. One night they ran out of drink.

"Mary'll fetch some," said the farmer, and he called her in. But when she came, she looked so young and small the others protested.

"You can't send a little scrap like that out in the dark!" said one of them. "She'll be scared to death."

"Not she!" said the farmer. "She's not afraid of anything – are you, Mary?"

"No, sir," answered Mary, whisking the dirty glasses away. "But if you want my advice, you'd be better off in your beds than wasting time with your old tales."

Still, she put on her hat and went down to the pub, through all the dark and the lonely lanes, and she came back without batting an eyelid.

That caused a lot of talk, but the farmer said, "That's nothing. She'd go anywhere on earth, day or night. I'll give a golden guinea to any man who can name something she's afraid to do."

"Done!" cried one of his friends. "I'll lay she daren't go down to the churchyard at night and bring us back a skull. There's never a girl in England who'd do that."

The farmer looked downcast and somebody said, "That's too much to ask, that is. Why, I wouldn't go myself, never mind a young lady."

"Well, we can put it to her," said the farmer, and he called her in again.

"Mary," he said, "they want you to go down to the churchyard to fetch us a skull. And it must be at night, mind."

"Day or night, it's all the same to me," said the dauntless girl. "But I'll want some time off in the afternoon to make up for working late. And I'll thank you to bid your guests drink up, master, before they think of any more jobs for me."

And she fixed them with such a look that they found themselves shuffling to their feet before they rightly knew what they were doing.

"Next week then, lads," cried the farmer. "At midnight. And you'll see whether she's afraid or no."

But the man who'd made the bet was aiming to win his money by fair means or foul and he offered the sexton five shillings to frighten her away. So a little before the time, the sexton unlocked the churchyard gate and hid behind one of the tombs.

It was very dark and creepy there, late at night. There were squeaks and cries and flutterings that made even him jump. Once he thought he glimpsed a white shape gliding across the grass and his heart hammered so fast he felt it would burst. It seemed a hard-earned five shillings and he was starting to regret it when he saw a light bobbing across the churchyard. It was Mary, as brisk and business-like as if she was going to market. She set her lantern down by a pile of old bones in the corner of the graveyard and began to sort through them till she found a skull. Now came the sexton's chance. Pitching his voice as deep and hollow as he could make it, he boomed out, "Let that be. It's my grandfather's skull-bone."

The dauntless girl gave a single sniff and put it aside. She'd sorted out a neat pile of thigh-bones when she came upon another skull. The sexton watched her take out a cloth to wipe the mud off before he cried, "And that one too! It's my grandmother's."

The dauntless girl glared in the direction of the tombstone.

"Be thankful it isn't yours!" she snapped. "I've put one back already and I'm not leaving two. Grandfather or grandmother, a skull I must have and that's my last word. Be off and haunt someone else."

And with that she slammed off, locking the churchyard gate behind her. So there was the sexton, locked in among the tombstones, while she took the skull back to her master.

"And a dirty old thing it is," she said, when she got home. "What you want with it is beyond me. As if I haven't got better things to do than traipse back and forth to the churchyard."

She was all for going to bed, but her master stopped her.

"Did you see anything?"

"What would I see in the middle of the night? I got mud all over my skirt, if that's what you mean."

"Didn't you hear anything?" asked the man who'd laid the bet.

"Oh yes!" she said. "Some old ghost was wittering on at me. First I couldn't have one skull, and then I couldn't have another. But I told him straight, 'Grandfather or grandmother,' I said, 'I must have a skull, and that's an end to it.' So I took one and locked the gate. He made a terrible to-do when I'd gone, banging and thumping to get out."

"I believe you!" said the man, and he clapped on his hat and ran off down to the churchyard as fast as his legs would carry him.

He had to knock up the vicar to get the key, and when they did get in, they couldn't see the sexton. They never would have found him, but that the vicar spotted two boots sticking out from behind a tombstone. The sexton had got himself in such a state, for fear of ghosts, that he'd fainted clean away. And he had a lot of explaining to do, when he recovered, because the vicar wanted to know what he was doing there all alone at dead of night.

The vicar wasn't best pleased when he got the story out of him but everyone else was very taken with it, and the news of the dauntless girl travelled far and wide. Before long the squire came riding by, asking to see her master.

"It's my mother," he said. "We buried her last autumn, and as nice a service as you could wish, but she will *not* lie easy. She came back before the week was out and she's been haunting us ever since. Now I don't mind the odd appearance, for old times' sake, but there's reason in all things and she turns up morning, noon and night. Mealtimes are worst. I tell you, the dinner doesn't go down right for looking at her. She always was an absent-minded body, but she's worse since she was ghosted. You try eating your dinner when the knife and fork opposite are bobbing up and down! You can't fancy it."

"Unsettling," agreed the farmer. "But where do I come in?"

"Well, the servants won't stay and I can't say I blame them. We lost the cook last week and I'd have sworn she was as steady as a rock. She went screeching out of the house like a scalded cat and all because Mother took it into her head to stir the soup. I haven't had a morsel fit to eat since, and the whole house is knee-deep in dust. I was wondering if your girl Mary could help me out. The word is she's a real dauntless girl so I daresay she could put up with Mother."

"We can ask her," said the farmer and he called her in and told her the whole story.

"What do you say?" he asked. "I'll not press you one way or the other."

"I don't set much store by ghosts," she said, "and I'm willing to go. But I think I should get a shilling or two extra to make up for the inconvenience. If that suits you, then I'll come."

So it was settled, and she went off with the squire that very day. She met with plenty of dark looks and darker murmurings, and she soon found there wasn't a soul would set foot in the house after dark, but she paid no heed to that. She went to work to get the house spick and span and before long it shone like a Christmas tree with all the polish. And every night she cooked a hearty meal for the squire and every night she laid two places – one for him, and one for the ghost. She always cooked enough for two and she made sure to help the ghost to vegetables and pass the salt and pepper. The ghost was pleased as punch, because nobody had ever waited on her before, and everything went like clockwork until one day the squire had to go off to London on business.

The next day Mary was having a good turn out when the ghost appeared. She was dressed all in black and she'd forgotten her head but that didn't bother Mary, who bade her a polite good morning.

"Mary," said the ghost. "Are you afraid of me?"

"No, ma'am," said Mary, dusting out the cupboard. "Why should I be? You're dead, aren't you?"

The ghost was a bit baffled by that and she came and went alarmingly for a minute or two. Then she said, "Well, you're a brave girl, and I want you to come down the cellar with me."

"Yes, ma'am," said Mary. "Will I get a lantern?"

"No, you won't need a light. I'll shine for you and you can see your way by that. Come along now."

There was a trap-door leading down to the cellar, and the ghost passed clean through it. Mary heaved it up and followed after. It was very dark inside and the steps were steep and slippery, but Mary picked her way as best she could, guided by the cold greenish glow of the ghost.

"Over here!" it cried. "And feel around on the floor. There's a loose tile."

Mary groped around in the dark and lifted up the tile. Under it there was something cold and soft.

"Take it out," said the ghost.

So Mary did as she was told, and when she lifted it, it chinked. It was a piece of leather and wrapped in the leather were two bags of coins, a big one and a little one.

"The big one's for my son," said the ghost. "And the little one's for you because you're a brave girl and you know how to behave to an old ghost."

With that she vanished and Mary was left alone in the dark. She had a hard time finding her way out into the light again, but as soon as she did, she took a look at the bags. They were both filled with gold.

When the squire got home next day she told him all that had happened.

"Here's the gold, master," she said. "And . . . " here she took a deep breath and looked him straight in the eye. "And the big bag's for me, and the little one's for you."

"Are you sure?" asked the squire. "Seems to me it's the wrong way round. I'd have expected the big bag, seeing I'm her son."

"Oh no," said Mary, lying in her teeth. "It's the other way about. Really!"

And she stuck to her story so firmly that he decided it must be true. But in the end it worked out all right, because he decided he'd marry her, seeing she was such a good cook, and pretty into the bargain. Of course, when they were man and wife, they shared the gold and it kept them very comfortably. But Mary made sure to cross the knives and forks to keep the old ghost away. And the squire never did learn the truth of the matter.

The Draiglin' Hogney

There was once a lord who had three sons. Fine brave young men they were, with blood as blue as ink and hearts as bold as lions. But they hadn't two pennies to rub together because their father had fallen on hard times and all their land was gone.

So the eldest brother decided to seek his fortune and he set off one day with his hawk and his hound and his white Arab charger. And he rode and he rode till he'd left his own country far behind him and he was in a land he'd never seen before. A dark forest stretched ahead of him and leading into the forest was a narrow track. It looked a strange, lonely sort of place, but the young man was looking for adventure so he turned his horse and rode in.

But it was very still under the trees and no sun shone. Even the birds were silent and the leaves seemed to be whispering to each other. The hound slunk along with its tail between its legs and the horse set its ears back and shied at every step.

After a while the quiet and the dark began to get the young man down too, and he was sickening for voices and company. Then, through the trees, he saw lights glinting.

He spurred the horse on and soon they came to a great clearing. Within it stood a palace, glittering with gold and silver and precious stones. The garden was set with fountains and flowering trees, and there were lights blazing at every window, but there wasn't a soul to be seen.

The young man knocked on the gate and it swung open, though no hand moved it. The horse could hardly be persuaded inside. He went on into the palace, while the hound whined and shivered. The floors were of marble and the horse's hooves rang out hard and loud.

He came at last to a great banqueting hall. A feast was laid out on gold and silver plates. There was roast pig and peacock and marzipan trifles, and the wine, which stood in tall silver flagons, was the finest he'd ever tasted. Food was laid out for the beasts, too – hay for the horse and meat for the hound and hawk. They were all very tired so they set to and ate and drank their fill.

It was very late by now and they were just settling down

to go to sleep when the clock struck twelve. On the last stroke the doors were flung open and into the hall strode the Draiglin' Hogney.

At the very sight of him, the dog's hackles rose, the horse reared and the hawk bated like a mad thing. But the young man, who was a kindly soul, said cheerfully, "I suppose we've got you to thank for our supper. Pull up a chair."

The Draiglin' Hogney made a horrible attempt at a smile and sat down by the fire. He looked at the furious beasts and said abruptly, "Does your hound bite?"

"Well . . . " said the young man, rather taken aback. "Sometimes."

"Throw this over him," said the Draiglin' Hogney. "That'll cure him."

He passed the young man a long hair and the eldest son, bewildered but polite, laced it into the hound's collar.

"It's very kind . . . " he began, but the Draiglin' Hogney barked, "And does your horse kick?"

"From time to time," said the young man, baffled.

"Take this."

He handed over another hair and the young man bound it into the horse's bridle.

"Does your hawk rend?"

"I wouldn't say *rend* exactly . . . "

"Does she or doesn't she? Yes or no?"

"Yes," said the young man.

"Here."

He produced a third hair which the young man twisted into the hawk's jesses.

"I really am most grateful," he said. "And after we've come in and eaten all your food too. But I don't think I know your name."

"I," said his host, "am the Draiglin' Hogney." His voice rose to a roar and all his whiskers bristled. "And when a stranger comes to my house, he never gets out alive!"

With that he whipped out a slim magician's rod and pointed it at the young man. The hound strained forward, the hawk screamed and the horse slashed with his hooves, but the hairs tightened round them like chains and they were held fast. As for the young man, he fell senseless to the floor and that was the last he knew.

His father and two brothers waited and waited for the eldest son to return. But spring and summer went by and still he didn't come back. So the middle brother decided to go in search of the first and took his horse and his hound and his hawk and rode off till he too came to the forest and the deserted palace. He ate his fill in the banqueting hall and had just settled down to sleep when midnight struck and the Draiglin' Hogney appeared.

Now the second brother was just as friendly as the first and he saw nothing wrong with the Draiglin' Hogney, even if he did have fangs hanging down to his chest. He paid no heed to the snarls of his hound or the screams of his hawk and he bound them all up with the magic hairs.

But then the Draiglin' Hogney laughed horribly and cried, "Your brother is already in my power and now I have you too!" and he pointed his magician's staff and the middle brother fell to the floor senseless. And though the animals screamed with fury, the hairs held them in and they were helpless.

The third son waited alone with his father until it was plain his brothers would not return. Then he took *his* horse and his hound and his hawk and set off in his turn. He found the forest all right but, being a careful man by nature, would have skirted it. But then it occurred to him that it was the very place for an adventure so, knowing his brothers, he rode in.

He came to the palace and the banqueting hall where the feast lay ready. Though he was very hungry, he

wouldn't touch a crumb because he decided the whole place reeked of magic and he had no wish to be turned into a toad. So he made his supper off a bit of bread and cheese of his own bringing and settled down to wait.

Sure enough, midnight struck and the Draiglin' Hogney appeared. Now the youngest brother was friendly all right, but he was nobody's fool and he spotted the fangs straight away, *and* the long sharp claws, too. But he greeted his host pleasantly enough and they settled down by the fire for a chat.

"Does your horse kick?" demanded the Draiglin' Hogney.

"No," said the young man, promptly. "Never."

"Liar!" cried the Draiglin' Hogney. "There isn't a horse on earth that never kicks."

"Mine doesn't."

"Humph! Well, you're to wrap this round his bridle."

The young man knew there must be something special about the hair but he took it and pretended to twist it round the bridle. But as he returned to his chair he dropped it in the fire. To his dismay, it gave a loud crack and the Draiglin' Hogney jumped.

"What was that?"

"Just a bit of green wood," said the young man.

"Maybe," muttered the Draiglin' Hogney. "And maybe not. Does your hound bite?"

"Never."

"You're an impudent fool and deceitful to boot. Put this round his collar."

So the young man fiddled with the collar and dropped the hair in the fire. It gave the most almighty crack and the Draiglin' Hogney started.

"Green wood," said the young man. "What's the hair supposed to do?"

"Never you mind. No doubt you'll say your hawk never rends either, so I'll spare myself the question. This is for her jesses."

He passed over a third hair, which the young man again dropped in the fire. It sounded like the crack of doom and the Draiglin' Hogney shot a good foot out of his chair.

"You should see your wood's seasoned better," said the young man. "That's the third time that's happened."

"Well, you'll never hear a fourth because I'm the Draiglin' Hogney and I'm going to put you with your brothers!"

Out came the wand and the young man felt himself freeze. Try as he might, he could not move a muscle. The Draiglin' Hogney advanced, grinning horribly, but even as he did so, the hawk swooped at his head, the hound went for his throat and the horse struck him such a mighty blow he was knocked unconscious. The wand fell and the young man was released from his spell. He pointed the wand in his turn and at once the Draiglin' Hogney dissolved into thin air and went wailing off into outer darkness, never to trouble mankind again.

"And now," said the youngest son, "we must search for my brothers."

They hunted that palace from top to bottom. They found whole attics full of treasure and chests so stuffed with jewels that the lids wouldn't close. Three days and three nights it took and at last the hound sniffed out a little cellar underground with cobwebs round the door. There lay the two brothers, fast asleep, and many more besides. There must have been a score of young men, all richly dressed and strongly armed, and all defeated by the magic of the Draiglin' Hogney. So the youngest son awakened them with a touch of the magician's staff and sent them on their way, loaded with wealth.

And as for the brothers themselves, they took as much gold as they could carry and returned to their father's house. And there they lived, rich and happy, for the rest of their lives.

The Treasure Ghost of Fife

Jock Mackintosh was the laziest man in Scotland. He was probably the laziest man in the whole world. He was a small farmer by trade and he kept all his animals in the kitchen, to save going out to feed them. He only took a bath once a month and when he did, he kept his clothes on and washed them and himself at the same time. He lived on cold porridge, which was the easiest thing he could think of, and that porridge saucepan had never seen water in its life.

He lived alone, because all his relations had washed their hands of him, but early one afternoon, as he was lying in bed, a party of aunts and uncles descended on him. One of his cousins was getting married and they'd come to get him up. They plunged him under the pump and dragged him off to church, where he dozed very happily till the couple were made man and wife. He didn't mind much, because he was a peaceable sort of man and there was a good meal afterwards. But the trouble came when it was all over, because the guests scattered and he was left to find his own way home.

He sat down on the roadside and thought. His home lay four miles away and he'd never walked that far in his life. The very idea made his legs ache. So he waited, hoping that some kind soul would appear and offer him a lift. But everyone was indoors, for it was getting late, and the longer he waited, the colder he grew. There was no help for it. He must walk or freeze.

He set off, going very gingerly for fear of straining himself. Every little bank seemed like a mountain, and every pebble a boulder. But then, as he reached the top of one rise, puffing mightily, he saw a glimmer of light ahead.

Lights meant lifts to Jock Mackintosh, so he stepped forward quite briskly, afraid that it might disappear. But as he drew near he saw, to his disappointment, no sign of a horse or cart which might carry him home. The light was coming from a man.

Anyone but Jock would have spotted something wrong straight away. The man was deathly pale and he shone like a lantern. He wore, too, the saddest expression ever seen on a human face. But it didn't strike Jock as odd. Anyone would feel gloomy, stranded on a lonely road, miles from home. He did himself.

"Evening," he said hopefully. "Waiting for a lift, are you? Perhaps you're going my way."

The man turned to him, his sadness giving way to an astonished joy.

"You," he said, in a deep, hollow voice, "are the first person who has dared to speak to me in a century. For a hundred years I have been doomed to haunt this spot

waiting and praying for a traveller bold enough to greet me. And I tell you, there have been times when I thought that man would never come."

"A hundred years!" said Jock, and then he gave the stranger a very hard stare indeed. Of course, it was obvious when you looked.

"You're a ghost!" he said accusingly.

"I am. And I hold a secret which I will reveal to you. I will make you rich."

Now Jock had recognised him, he felt uneasy. He'd have run away, only he wasn't the running kind. So he shifted from one foot to the other and wished the ghost would go away.

"I can lead you to buried treasure up the mountain. Come with me and I will show you where to dig gold and silver beyond your wildest dreams."

Well, Jock wasn't much of a one for mountain climbing, let alone digging. But he didn't like to say so and he smiled nervously and murmured, "Very kind, I'm sure."

"You shall have a castle, carpeted with silk. You can have jewels fit for an emperor's ransom and servants to wait on you hand and foot. You can live in the lap of luxury."

"Servants?" said Jock. "To wait on me?"

"Of course. There are riches there beyond man's counting. You can buy anything your heart desires."

"Like a carriage?" said Jock. "So I needn't walk any more?"

"A dozen if you wish."

"One would be plenty. Take me to that treasure!"

"Not so fast. Come to this place again at sundown tomorrow, and I will show you where it is."

"I'll be there," said Jock. "And it'll be the last bit of walking I ever do."

"But wait. There is more. I am bound by certain

conditions. In short, no cock must crow at sunset tomorrow, nor any horn be blown. Make sure of this, for if you fail I must depart, taking the secret with me."

"But that's impossible!" protested Jock. "I can't keep all the cocks quiet. Let alone horns!"

"Those are the conditions. Until tomorrow then. Farewell."

With that the ghost vanished and Jock was left alone. He went on his way, thinking deeply and he didn't much like the end of his thoughts because it added up to a lot of hard work. The horn problem was worse than the cocks because every shepherd sounded off at sunset to call his flocks in. And he could see the only way to stop it was to visit each shepherd in turn and ask him not to. Which meant a lot more walking than Jock cared for.

For a moment he wondered if it was worth it. He was on the brink of giving up the whole idea. But then the memory of those servants returned. He need never do a hand's turn again. And still revelling in the thought, he arrived home, and went straight to bed to prepare himself for the day's work ahead.

Morning came and his bones ached from the four mile walk. They'd ache worse before evening but he daren't think about that. He set his teeth, crawled out of bed, and went visiting the crofters.

The first one wouldn't believe him to start with. He roared with laughter and called on his wife to share the joke. But he soon changed his tune when his wife pointed out that anything which got Jock Mackintosh up at daybreak must be serious. And if the tale was true, Jock would be a man worth knowing when his sacks of treasure were gathered in. So they agreed very readily to do as he asked and sped him on his way with a fine big breakfast inside him.

The second farmer didn't think much of his story either. Not to begin with. And he wasn't too keen on Jock, being a hard-working man himself, with no time for lie-abeds. In the ordinary way they were barely on speaking terms, but Jock was persuasive with his talk of treasure and at last he got his way.

"But if you're pulling my leg, Jock Mackintosh," said the farmer, "may the good Lord help you."

Jock was far too spent for jokes. He had another four farms and thirteen crofts to cover and time was short. He hurried on, up the mountain, to get a promise from old Campbell the shepherd. But when he reached the lonely hut, old Campbell wasn't there.

And so it went on, all day. He had a terrible time, walking up hill and down dale, with never a minute to himself. By evening he was so tired to could cry. But he'd done it. He'd visited every farmyard in earshot and won a promise at each that the cocks would be kept indoors and the shepherds would stay silent.

Of course, his reputation helped. The crofters knew full well that he wouldn't stir a step unless it was life or death and that saved him some trouble convincing them. But it had been a backbreaking day for all that and only the thought of the treasure kept him going. And even its magic was wearing thin. If it took much digging, thought Jock, wiping the sweat from his brow, he'd almost rather let it be.

As he got to the crossroads, he saw the ghost shining in the dusk.

"You have kept my conditions?"

"I have," said Jock. "To the letter."

"You will be repaid. Now listen . . . "

Dark was falling and the road was quite silent. Now was the time when the cocks crowed, but there wasn't a sound. Every last one of them was penned up in a farmhouse kitchen, muffled in blankets to silence its call. As for the shepherds, their dogs were running like mad things to round up the sheep without the help of a horn.

"You will find the treasure," the ghost began, "up the mountain, two miles from . . . "

And then, out of the dusk, a horn sounded. Old Campbell, late and in a hurry, was leading his flock back over the hill. And the call sounded to Jock Mackintosh loud as the crack of Doom.

"You have failed the condition!" cried the ghost. "I can help you no more."

"Wait!" called Jock. "You can't not tell me."

"It is not permitted. Farewell."

Already the ghost was fading. For a moment its form hung in the air, faint as mist and then it had dissolved, leaving no trace behind.

"Farewell!" it called again. "Farewell."

And it was gone as if it had never been.

As for Jock Mackintosh, he sat down on a stone and cried for all his work and his blisters. And there was worse to come. Because he still had a long way to walk and never a sign of a lift.

But being an easiful soul, he cheered up presently.

"After all," he said to himself, plodding homewards, "two miles up the mountain is a long hard haul and like as not digging at the end of it. And they say money can be a terrible worry so I'm probably better off without it."

But he never got a chance to find out for he stayed a poor man for the rest of his life. And never again did he get up before daybreak.

The Dead Moon

A long time ago, before the days of electricity and good roads, the Lincolnshire Cars were criss-crossed with bogs. They were swampy and dangerous marshes and you had to know your way about or you'd fall into a patch of sinking mud and never come out alive. But if they were dangerous by day, they were much worse at night. Because bogles and evil things lived in the Cars and they came prowling out at night to lie in wait for passing travellers. There were will o' wisps which led a man astray and ghouls that gibbered and shrieked. And there were Dead Men's Fingers whose touch was cold as ice. They all came out on moonless nights and scrabbled round the cottages till the people of the Cars shut their doors and windows tight and prayed for a full moon. For the dark creatures of the Cars hated the moon. Her bright light hurt them.

Now when the moon learned what was happening in the Cars while she was away, she grew very angry and determined to put a stop to it. So one night, she wrapped herself in a thick black cloak and, hiding her shining hair beneath a dark hood, stepped down from the sky and came walking across the fens.

It was very dark in the Cars and all her brightness was hidden. There were shadows everywhere and voices crying. But she went on bravely, stepping lightly across tussocky grass and quaking mud. And as she walked deeper and deeper into the swamps, witches rode beside her, mounted on great black cats with shining eyes. They shrieked at her and crooked their fingers but they dared not touch her because of the little silvery light which spilled out from under her hood. Then came the skeletons, dancing and chattering their teeth at her like angry monkeys, and coal-black bogles too, but none could touch her. Spiteful brambles clawed at her with their hooked thorns, and cold fingers brushed against her cloak but no evil thing dared come nearer because of the light which spilled out from beneath her cloak.

But then, as she walked across the Cars, a stone turned under her foot and she put out a hand to save herself. As soon as she touched the ground, a bramble reached up and wound itself around her fingers, holding her fast.

While she was struggling to free herself, she heard a voice crying in the dark. It was a traveller. He'd got himself lost from the path and the will o' wisps had lured him further and further into the swamps. He was worn out and despairing and the shadows were gathering around him, ready to make an end of it. The moon could see the dead fingers reaching up for him, and the witches hovering nearby, and she grew so angry and sorry that she determined to save him.

She couldn't free herself from the brambles but she flung back her head and the hood fell off and all her light streamed out into the blackness. The dark things cowered back and the traveller saw the true path shining ahead of him. He struck out for it at once, all his weariness forgotten, and was soon on safe ground again.

But as for the moon, she could find no safety. The creeping, sucking plants sprang up to bind her and the harder she struggled, the tighter they held her. And as the night went on, she grew tired. The black things held back at first, frightened by her light. But little by little, as her struggles grew weaker, her hood fell forwards again, quenching her brightness, until at last there was darkness in the Cars. Then they fell on her and took her prisoner.

All through the night they yelled and stamped in triumph because they'd captured the moon and there was nothing left to withstand them. They quarrelled all night about how they should kill her but when the first grey light of morning came, they grew frightened and thrust her down into a deep pool and dropped a great flat stone on top to hold her fast. They set two will o' wisps to guard her and slunk back to their own dark holes to wait out the day.

Next night, the people of the Cars watched for the moon, but she never came, and the things of the bog roamed free. And as dark night after dark night passed,the bogles grew bolder. They came stalking among the houses, tapping at the windows and yelling to get in. No one dared set foot in the bogs for the sake of their lives, but still the moon did not return to protect them. And at last the people of the Cars began to fear she never would come back.

So they went to a wise woman to find out what had happened. But though she searched with book and crystal and brewing pot she could see nothing but darkness. So she told them to put straw and salt and a button by their doors and bring her any news they might hear.

Of course, the people talked about it by their firesides and out of doors wherever they met, until presently one man said, "I reckon I know where the moon is, though I was too frightened to think of it."

And he told them of how he got lost in the bogs one night and how the moon shone her light to bring him home again.

So back they went to the wise woman and she looked in her crystal. And this time, though the ball was dark as smoke, in the centre was a glimmer of light and she guessed what had happened.

"Are you sure you dare to seek the moon?" she asked. "It will be very dangerous."

"We must," they said. "The bogles are rattling at our doors now and the shadows come out even before dusk."

"Then you must go into the bogs at night," said the wise woman. "You must put a stone in your mouth and a hazel twig in your hand and you must speak no word aloud till you're safe home again. Look for a tombstone and a cross and a candle and there the moon will be."

Well, they were very frightened of the marsh at night but the men knew things would never be right till they got the moon back. Their women cried and begged them to stay safe at home but the very next night they set out.

It was quiet in the boglands. Each man carried a lantern and the dark things crowded outside the light, muttering and shuffling. Cold hands brushed them and mud sucked at their feet but they went on, further and further, speaking not a word. They were very much afraid.

Then they stopped. Before them was a deep pool and half in and half out of the water lay a long flat slab for all the world like a tombstone. A crooked branch formed a cross above it and a will o' wisp flickered on either side. So they knew they'd found the place and they knelt down and said the Lord's Prayer, silently because of what the wise woman had told them. Next they set their hands to the stone. Down swooped the bogles, ghouls, jack o' lanterns and all, screaming and chittering, but they dared not come too close because of the Lord's Prayer. The men heaved up the stone and as it rose they glimpsed a strange, beautiful face looking up at them. A dazzle of light shot up to the sky and all the horrors shrieked in dismay and scuttled back to their holes. Then the moon was shining down from the heavens and the path showed clear as day.

So for ever after the moon has shone her best in the Cars because she knows all about the evil things that live there, and she remembers how the men of the Cars went out to find her when she lay buried there.

Joe and the Sister Ghosts

Joe Reardon was only a scrawny little scrap of a lad and he hadn't had much of a life for himself since his mother died. His father had married again and his stepmother hated the sight of him, and grudged every penny he cost. She'd have got rid of him if she could, but she knew his father wouldn't stand for that. So she gave Joe all the dirty jobs to do and as little to eat as she dared.

Now it so happened there was a ghost that haunted the hills four miles away. It was a nasty sort of ghost. They said nobody who met it ever lived to tell the tale, and the stepmother thought it sounded just the thing to settle Joe. So she persuaded her husband to send him out to the smithy late one winter afternoon. The only way back from the smithy was past the haunted spot and the ghost came out at night.

"The plough chains need mending," said Joe's father, "and the wife says they can't wait. You're to take them straight away."

"But it's late!" Joe protested.

"And what of it?" the stepmother demanded. "You're not afraid of the dark are you – a boy of your age?"

"Now then," said his father. "Steady on, Eileen. That's a nasty spot at night and I don't blame the lad if he's qualmish. He can go in the morning."

Joe flushed. "I'm not scared," he said. "I'll go now. And I'll be back by midnight, or not at all."

It was late when he got to the forge and the job took a long time.

"You'd best stay the night," said the blacksmith. "You don't want to take that road in the dark."

But Joe shook his head. "I said I'd be back before midnight and I'll be as good as my word."

By the time he set off, it was night and there wasn't a glimmer to light his way. He fell to thinking of Tim Murphy, who had taken that road before him, and never came back. But he wasn't going to be beaten, and he walked on, swinging the plough chains and singing to himself in a small unsteady voice.

He'd got about two miles from the forge when he came to the top of a hill. The road stretched ahead, very lonely in the darkness, and a great stone reared up out of the ground. Tim Murphy had been found by that stone.

Joe didn't feel like singing any more. He wanted to take to his heels. But he gripped the plough chains and went on as firmly and steadily as he could.

He hadn't gone a dozen paces when the ghost fell on him. He sensed bat wings swooping over him, and then he was fighting for his life. Claws raked him and great blows buffeted him but when he tried to hit back there was nothing to get hold of. And the earth itself seemed to join in the battle. Dust rose up to blind him and stone sucked itself out of the earth and flung itself at his head so fast he barely had time to dodge.

A chasm opened before his feet, set with teeth of ice. The black-winged creature swooped down, driving him to the brink. But Joe lashed at it with the plough chains, the shadow melted and the chasm closed like a mouth.

He only had a second to catch his breath before it was on him again, wrapping him round with leathery wings. The cold of its touch struck him to the bone and he swung the plough chains with all his might. He heard a cry, felt the grip slacken and suddenly the monster lay still.

Joe wasted no time in triumph. He wrapped the plough chains round it and pulled it to its feet. It followed him as quietly as a bridled horse and he led it home to his father's house. His stepmother was sitting up, planning what she'd do now he was gone, and when she saw him, she let out a shriek.

"Joe! I thought the ghost had got you!"

"Bad luck for you it didn't!" said Joe and he loosed its chains and set it free. It went for his stepmother like a whirlwind. It beat her black and blue and when at last she broke free, she rushed from the house, yelling as if all the devils in hell were after her. As well she might. It took Joe an hour to clear up the kitchen, but it was worth it.

When it was all put to rights, he set the table and made himself some supper. The ghost was standing by the door.

"Eat," he said.

"No," answered the ghost, "but I'd beg a favour. Come

with me tomorrow night and fight my sister. She's bigger than me, and fiercer, but if you win, it will be worth your while."

"That I will," said Joe, "and I'll bring the plough chains."

So next evening, fortified by two breakfasts, a double dinner and six eggs for tea, Joe set out to meet the ghost again. She was waiting in the usual place and she led him along the road till they came to a haunted wood, dark with pine trees. It was quieter in that wood than any place had a right to be, and he shivered with cold. And then, in a patch of shadow, he saw the second ghost waiting.

Joe gripped his plough chains tight and stood ready. She turned herself into a giant snake and came oozing towards him, forked tongue flickering. Joe had always hated snakes.

One great coil looped out and seized him, squeezing him so tight he could feel the bones crack. But he worked his hands free and twisted the tip of its tail till the grip loosened. So she became an eagle and plunged on him, clawing for his eyes. He flung up one hand to guard his face, and with the other lashed out the plough chains and she screamed and flew clear. She turned on him again in the shape of a dragon, and he was scorched and blinded by the flames, but he managed to fling the chains round her neck and bind her fast. And then she grew still and he knew he'd won.

Back to his father's house he went, with the two ghosts trotting behind, quiet as cats. They found his stepmother barring the door against him and Joe set the ghosts on her and drove her out. They settled down to supper, but neither of the ghosts would eat and presently the second one said, "We have a sister, stronger and fiercer than either of us. Will you fight her? There's treasure in it."

Joe said, "I've no need for treasure and I'm tired of

fighting. I've got bruises to show for it already. Why should I come?"

"You must," they said. "For our sakes."

"Well," said Joe, "you've put paid to my stepmother, for which I'm very grateful. And though you did set on me, I'm sure there was no ill will in it."

"None in the world," said the ghosts. "We're as tired of fighting as you are and if you'll just do as we ask this once, we'll be free of it forever."

"Very well," said Joe. "I'll meet you tomorrow. But this

must be the last time, mind."

"If you win," they said, "it will be."

So next night, Joe set off for the wood and found the two sister ghosts waiting for him. They led him through the trees till they came to a ruined castle. Joe had lived in those parts all his life but he'd never heard tell of that castle before. And he didn't like it now. The very smell of it made his hair prickle and there was a waiting feeling that made him wish he'd stayed home.

Then, like a thunderclap, the last of the sister ghosts fell upon him. She was taller than the tallest tree and colder than midwinter. She fought in silence and struggle though he might, Joe knew she was too strong. Her cold hands gripped his throat and he couldn't lift a finger to save himself. It was all over and there was nothing he could do.

But just as he was giving up, the grip loosened. His enemy had turned aside. The second of the sister ghosts had come to Joe's aid. She cried "Help me!" and Joe came to his senses again and struck out with the plough chains.

But the last of the sister ghosts was far stronger than the others. She flinched briefly at the touch of the iron chains and then turned herself into a wall of fire. It wrapped Joe round, blinding and burning him. The plough chains glowed red hot and with a cry he dropped them. His last defence was gone, and the flames blazed high.

And now the first sister came to the rescue. Her icy coldness quenched the flames and Joe had a moment's grace to recover the chains. He flung them at the fire and it became a rock. So Joe bound it tight, and suddenly the fight was over.

"Well!" he said, gasping for breath. "That was touch and go."

He looked round and saw three beautiful young girls

standing in the castle ruins. The youngest and most beautiful of them all was bound by the plough chains.

"You have saved us all," she said. "I did my sisters a great wrong and because of it we were doomed to haunt the land and fight with every passer-by. Only a man without fear could free us. You have released us now and in return we will reward you."

She led him through a broken gate to a pit in the ground which had once been a strong room. A rusty chest stood in one corner, half hidden by grass and weeds. But the lid opened smooth as silk and inside there was treasure fit for a king.

"Take it," she said. "We quarrelled over it once but now it has no value for us. Take it, and with it our blessings."

Her voice faded and the ghosts were gone. Joe stood alone in the moonlight, gazing at the treasure.

He took it home and used it to build a fine big house for himself. He married the prettiest girl in the county and they had ten children, all as good as gold and beautiful as the day. And as for the wicked stepmother, they never saw her again.

Tammy and the Trolls

Up in the hills in the Shetland Isles, there once lived three trolls. Now trolls are nasty creatures to meet and these three were no exception. There was Molly, who had a nose like a walking stick, and Milly, who was as thin as a runner bean, and Minnie, who was the size of a haystack. They lived together in a tumbledown cottage high on a hill and all the children for miles around were warned never, never to go near that hill for fear the trolls would get them. The trolls were fond of children. Cooked.

But there was one young lad called Tammy who lived in the village at the foot of Troll Hill. Heedless as a grasshopper he was. He never listened to a word anyone said.

"Keep away from the beehives," said his father, but Tammy wouldn't and he got stung.

"Mind you don't climb the elm tree," said his brother. "It's rotten." But Tammy climbed it and it broke.

"Don't go near the stream," said his mother, but Tammy

did, and he fell in and caught his death of cold.

His friends and relations could talk themselves blue in the face but Tammy always knew best.

One day Tammy took his ball out into the fields. He kicked it here and there, aimlessly, until he noticed the ground was getting very steep. When he looked back, he found his house lay a long way behind him and he'd got himself half way up Troll Hill. Any other boy would have picked up that ball and run, but not Tammy. He didn't believe in trolls. So he went on kicking and climbing until he came to the top of the hill. There was a rickety, tumbledown house on the hill-top and inside he could hear someone singing.

"Buckets of blood and roasted boys," sang a hoarse, raspy voice. "Boil them quick to stop their noise."

Tammy stopped. It wasn't the kind of song his mother sang, but it sounded cheerful. And he was very thirsty after his long climb. So without a moment's thought, he knocked on the door and went inside.

In the kitchen, Lucky Minnie was making bone broth. But when she saw Tammy, she stopped and smiled. The smile showed bright green teeth, filed neatly into points. A huge black troll dog sat by the fire. Its eyes were red as coals and when it saw Tammy it snarled.

"Quiet!" said Lucky Minnie, and kicked it. She sidled up to Tammy and pinched him hard.

"Nice and plump," she said. "Just the thing for our tea."

"Wait a minute!" cried Tammy.

"Fried in butter," added Lucky Minnie, "with a sprig of parsley."

"Oh no you don't!" said Tammy, and made a dash for the door. But before he'd gone two paces, the troll dog had risen, with a growl, to block his path, and Lucky Minnie picked him up by the scruff of the neck and dropped him in a sack. She hung it on a hook by the door and beamed at him.

"You bide quiet, my little chickabiddy," she said, "and I'll make a nice bit of stuffing to go with you."

"You're not going to eat me, are you?" said Tammy, shocked.

"And why not, dearie? You'll be tender as a young rabbit, I'll be bound."

"No I won't," said Tammy. "I'm tough and horrible and I'll give you stomach ache."

Lucky Minnie laughed till her teeth rattled.

"Bless him!" she said. "They all say that, dearie. You'll make a supper fit for a king. No, don't struggle!" she added, as Tammy squirmed inside his sack. "You'll spoil your flavour."

Tammy watched her sharpen her knife and get out the big frying pan. Just as she was coming towards him he said, "I'd go better in a pie – if you've got an onion, that is."

She hesitated, and he added, "My mother says the meat's tastier that way."

"Aye," she said, "but a pie's more trouble. Still . . . Milly's awful fond of them. I'll do it! Now, you bide here while I fetch the onion."

"You'll need a bayleaf as well, and a bit of sage," said Tammy, to give himself more time.

"You won't go sneaking off, while my back's turned?"

"As if I would!" said Tammy.

"Anyway," said Lucky Minnie, "if you tried, my dog would tear you in pieces. Back in a minute."

The second she was out of the door, Tammy began squirming and wriggling like an eel. The sack was tied tight round his neck but he was thin and strong and bit by bit he got one hand out, and began to pick the ropes loose. He looked at the troll dog which had been left to guard him. It was lying by the fire, gazing into the flames.

With another great heave he'd got one shoulder free and he caught hold of the hook on which the sack was hung and pulled himself up. The troll dog sprang to its feet, snarling horribly, and stalked across to him. Its red eyes flamed and its back bristled.

But Tammy pulled out his ball and flung it hard through the open door. The troll dog bounded after it and in that moment Tammy leapt to the ground and snatched up a big iron ladle. Back came the troll dog growling worse than ever, and Tammy knocked it cold with his ladle, then picked it up and stuffed it into the sack in his place.

He could hear Lucky Minnie humming outside and he hurriedly gathered up all the cups and saucers he could find and flung them in the sack on top of the troll dog. The sack looked a bit bumpy but he thought it would fool her. And now he could hear her heavy footsteps, so he jumped behind the door just as she reappeared.

She stumped over to the bag and poked it.

"You in there!" she shouted. "Do I mince you, or cut you in collops?"

No answer came from the bag, so she thumped it.

"It's no good sulking, laddie!" she shouted. "Just think of the pleasure you'll be giving me and my sisters."

Still there was no reply and she seized the ladle and struck the bag hard. There was a terrible crash of breaking crockery and a yelp from the unhappy troll dog.

"Stop your havering!" she shouted. "How am I to cook you if you won't give me the recipe?"

She walloped the sack again and there was a deafening smash and a howl. In the confusion, Tammy took his chance. He slipped out of the open door and away down the hillside as fast as his legs would carry him.

But Minnie had eyes like a hawk and she spotted the

movement. She came hurling down the slope after him, arms threshing like windmills.

"Stop! Stop!" she shouted. "We want you for our tea!"

Away went Tammy, as if the devil was after him. He plunged down the hillside like a deer, but she was faster. She was gaining on him.

At the foot of the hill lay a stream, crossed by a dozen stepping stones. As Tammy set foot on the first stone, he could hear Lucky Minnie hard behind him. He skipped across those stones faster than thought, but when he got to the seventh, she lunged forward and seized him. He twisted free and heard her cry out. The stones were slippery and she'd lost her footing. She teetered for a minute, flailing the air, and then crashed into the running water. Her arms churned the water to foam as she vanished from sight.

As for Tammy, he went on home, and glad he was to get there. But the water of that stream runs white with foam to this very day. And they say Lucky Minnie is still down there churning.

Lucott the Pirate

Lucott was a pirate and he wasn't one of the dashing golden-hearted kind, either. He was black-browed and black-bearded and he had a black temper to match. He and his crew harried the Somerset coast with the skull and crossbones flying and many a prisoner walked the frisky plank when Black Lucott's men were hunting. He had gold by the sackful, taken from rich merchantmen and he hoarded it in a chest in Porlock harbour. The people of Porlock spoke softly to him when he came ashore, because of his treasure and his men's sharp cutlasses, but there wasn't a soul in the port didn't breathe a sigh of relief when they saw him leave harbour and put to sea again.

Well, years went by and Lucott grew crueller and fiercer with every one that passed. There were plenty of brave men tried to put a stop to him but he had a good ship and a well-trained crew and he always got away scot free. But he met his match at last in a French privateer. He fought it out from morning till night, broadside to broadside with all guns blazing, but at the end of the day, Lucott's vessel sank to the bottom of the sea and every hand went with her.

When the people of Porlock learnt that Lucott was dead they were pleased and relieved. They held a service to settle his soul and then they shared out his treasure and thought they'd heard the last of him. But they were out of luck.

Next morning the Sunday bells rang out and everybody in Porlock put on gloves and hats and set off for church. All went well until the parson mounted the steps to the pulpit to give the sermon. Then, all of a sudden, there was a sound like a thunderclap as the door burst open. A huge, black-bearded figure came stamping up to the altar. Lucott had returned from the dead.

There was pandemonium in the church. Children were shrieking, young ladies fainting, and the butcher's wife fell into hysterics. The parson hammered on the pulpit till his hands were sore but all to no purpose. It was the organist who saved the day. He played such a mighty chord that the uproar was drowned and the church fell silent.

The parson glared at Lucott and pointed a shaking finger.

"Out!" he said. "This is no place for you."

But Lucott threw back his head and laughed.

"Why not?" he asked dangerously. "If I've a fancy to come to church, you can't stop me."

With that he strolled over to the front pew and settled himself comfortably.

"Carry on!" he said. "Don't mind me. I like a bit of preaching."

So the parson gathered his wits together and went on. But it was a poor sort of sermon he gave and the last hymn was a disgrace. Nobody could hit their top notes with Lucott sitting there. They gave it up as a bad job and scrapped the last verse altogether. And after the parson gave the blessing, you couldn't see them for dust. Mrs Wilkin's hat was squashed flat as a pancake in the scrimmage and even the vicar was reeling.

"You'll have to lay him, sir," said the people's warden. "We can't go through that again."

But the parson looked doubtful. "I don't know how!" he protested. "What if he won't go?"

"You must make him. Show him who's master."

The parson shook his head. "Not without help. Find me eleven other clergymen and I'll have a go, but do it on my own I will not. It's asking too much."

Everyone agreed that was fair and next day the church wardens set out to look for eleven more parsons. It wasn't easy. News of Lucott's ghost had already spread and word was out that he'd be a hard soul to lay.

"I doubt if I can help," said the vicar of Crowcombe politely. "I've not got a lot of experience of this type of work. And they say Oxford men are best anyway. I'm Cambridge myself."

"I'm too old for the job," mumbled old Canon Truebody from Wells. "You need strong young fellers who ain't afraid of a scrap."

"Too busy," said the new curate of Porlock Weir. "Try Glastonbury."

They did try Glastonbury. They tried every parish in Somerset. They scoured the whole countryside and at that they had a job to muster twelve. But one cold morning in February, a dozen pale and nervous clergymen gathered outside Porlock church. Each carried a Bible and a candle and they all looked as if they'd very much rather be elsewhere.

"Come on," said the archdeacon of Bristol, squaring his

shoulders. "Let's get it over."

He marched into the church, gripping his candle so tight it squashed out of shape. The others shuffled after him, their footsteps echoing on the stone floor. One or two lingered on the threshold.

"Lucott!" shouted the archdeacon. "Show yourself!"

Eerie laughter rang round the church, but the ghost did not appear. The clergymen felt a cold wind whipping their robes and the candles flickered madly.

"Lucott!" cried the archdeacon again. "Come out!"

There was a bloodcurdling shriek and all the candles went out. The church bells rang wildly and then, just as suddenly, fell silent.

"For the last time, Lucott, are you coming or not?"

"I am coming!" called a tremendous voice, and with a swoop a vast shadow was upon them – a shadow so cold that its very touch chilled them.

It was too much. The archdeacon stood his ground, but even he couldn't steady his companions. Someone broke away, dropping book and candle in a rush to escape. Suddenly it was a rout. Everyone was caught up in the panic and within seconds, only the ghost remained within Porlock Church.

The villagers were very dashed when they heard what had happened.

"Seems to me it's a parson's job!" said some. "If they won't take him on, who will?"

But then, as the blacksmith pointed out, it was one thing to talk about ghost laying, and quite another to do it – especially when the ghost was Black Lucott. So they thanked the clergymen kindly for their trouble and thought none the worse of them.

But the story went round and by and by, the vicar of Watchet got wind of it. He was a hard-riding,drinking sort of parson and he'd missed his chance at Lucott because it was a hunting day. When he heard the story he was furious.

"Impudence!" he said. "Sheer insolence. I'll teach that ghost manners."

He called all the clergymen together and gave them a tremendous talking to.

"You're letting him think he's won," he said. "But we'll show him better. I want the whole pack of you up at the church tomorrow and we'll see who chases who out of it."

"But you don't understand," said the young curate of West Zoyland nervously. "He really is very powerful. Quite frankly, I wouldn't care to face him again."

"Very well," said the vicar of Watchet. "Then I'll go in on my own and the rest of you can follow later. But I'll expect you outside the church at nine o'clock sharp."

Well, the vicar of Watchet had a fierce way of looking at you and somehow none of the other clergymen cared to argue. So at nine o'clock on the dot they came together, books and candles at the ready.

"Right," said the vicar. "You wait here. If I'm not out by ten you're to come in and get me."

They nodded nervously and watched him enter. At first they could only hear his voice, calling loudly and impatiently for the ghost.

"I do wish he'd be careful," murmured the curate of West Zoyland. "Lucott isn't a hunt servant, after all."

And indeed it did sound as if the ghost had taken offence for all of a sudden there came such a screech that their hair stood on end. But as it died away, they heard the vicar's voice, rising to a roar.

"Will you hold your tongue! And stop flapping that cloak about *at once!*"

His voice dropped to a mumble and there was no more from the ghost. After a little while, some of the bolder sort crept closer. But they still couldn't hear properly so they jumped up and peered through one of the stained glass windows to find out what was going on.

The scene took their breath away. There was the vicar of Watchet, thumbs in waistcoat pockets, holding forth like the village schoolmaster. And there was the ghost, slumped down in a pew, scowling, mutinous, but quiet. The vicar seemed to be putting it through an examination.

"Now . . . " came his voice clearly. "Answer me this. How many angels can stand on the head of a pin?"

Lucott's face twisted with the effort of thought. His great fists clenched and he flushed scarlet.

"How would I know?" he muttered at last. "Let me be."

"Oh no," cried the vicar. "If you can't answer, you're in my power. That's the rule. You there!" he called to one of the watchers. "Fetch me a donkey as quick as you can. We've got him now."

So somebody ran off to find a donkey while Lucott's ghost and the Watchet vicar glared at each other. When it arrived, the vicar said sharply, "Get on it, Lucott, and be quick about it."

"Not I!" said Lucott. "A flea-bitten little neddy! I want a horse."

"Well, you're not getting one. You failed my question so now you must do as you're told. You'll get on that donkey and you'll ride to Watchet with me."

For one long minute it looked as if Lucott would rebel. The watching parsons held their breath and the vicar of Watchet stood like a statue. Then Lucott broke. With a snarl of rage he mounted the donkey and off they went.

All the way to Watchet they rode, with Lucott grumbling at every step. The vicar said in a low voice, "He's in an ugly mood. Someone had better go ahead to warn everyone to keep clear. I don't want anybody on the street when he arrives."

The people of Watchet needed no persuading. By the time the party got there, every street was deserted, and every door closed. Little children had been snatched inside and the shopkeepers had shuttered their windows. There wasn't a soul to be seen.

But one man hadn't listened to the warning. Tom Paxton, the biggest gossip in Somerset, was waiting in hiding behind the rocks on the seashore. He hadn't bothered to get indoors, because he always thought he knew best, and now he was waiting for a glimpse of the famous Porlock ghost.

Down the silent streets rode the vicar, with the donkey shambling behind him. When they reached the seashore, the vicar raised his arms, ready to return Lucott to the depths. But just as he did so, the old pirate spotted Paxton.

"Avast there! A spy! I'll teach you to pry into my affairs if it's the last thing I do!"

Before the vicar could stop him, he swept down on Paxton and struck him such a blow he fell senseless. He was bending to finish his work when the vicar called out in a voice like thunder.

"Down!" he cried. "Down to the bottom of the sea and never come back again."

And down Lucott went, as if that last rebellion had worn him out. There was a cry, a great splash and that was the end of him. The vicar went back to Watchet and the Porlock people took up their affairs again. But they didn't forget Lucott. They never have. And to this day, if you go to Porlock, they'll tell you the tale of the laying of the pirate's ghost.

Look carefully at the borders. Every one is different!